Eden Springs

G. Roger Corey

HARVEST HOUSE PUBLISHERS
Eugene, Oregon 97402

Eden Springs

Copyright © 1999 by G. Roger Corey
Published by Harvest House Publishers
Eugene, Oregon 97402

Library of Congress Cataloging-in-Publication Data

Corey, G. Roger, 1951 –
  Eden Springs / G. Roger Corey.
      p. cm.
  ISBN 0-7369-0105-1
  1. Title.
  PS3553.06465S66 1999
  813'.54—dc21

                                    99-14229
                                    CIP

Printed in the United States of America.

99 00 01 02 03 04 / BC / 10 9 8 7 6 5 4 3 2 1

For Claudia

Acknowledgments

I would like to thank Major Steve "Sly" Lyzenga for his assistance with technical portions of this book related to flying. I am also grateful to Karen Stegner, Deb Lara, and Greg Tamblyn for their encouragement and support.

Expecting always
Some brightness to hold in trust,
Some final innocence
Exempt from dust,
That, hanging solid,
Would dangle through all.

Stephen Spender

*"He will deliver
one who is not innocent,
And he will be delivered
through the cleanness
of your hands."*

JOB 22:30

One

~

S ome people hold sensitivity like a lantern before
them as they move through life, and it only takes
one glance to know how they will react to any
given situation. With others, however, this quality is
masked behind something elusive, and you are never
quite certain where they, or you, stand. This is how I felt
about Richard Taggart when he returned to Eden Springs
from the Gulf War. We were not exactly a sleepy little
community on the banks of the Missouri river—this was
due to our close proximity to Emerson Air Force Base—
but we were provincial, and Tag had just been overseas. I
had known him since childhood, and although I could not
at first comprehend the evasiveness of his actions, he did
return with that same intensity of gaze—the set mouth,
the furrowed brow—as if something important or necessary always conjured in the depths of his thoughts.

As with most childhood friends, we had chosen different courses in life which had set us apart geographi-
cally, if not emotionally. Tag had spent two years in a
junior college studying—either I cannot recall or he was
an undeclared major—and I had prepared to enter a Bible
seminary. Neither of us had followed through on our
plans, however, and after a few semesters Tag had joined

the Air Force, and I had gone on to complete a degree in English. After graduation, I was offered a position as a reporter on the Eden Springs Banner. It was a good newspaper, respected in the community, and I was proud of my job. But it wasn't the job for which I felt that God had called me. I believe now that there are many times in life when we let our feelings of inadequacy hinder the plans God has for us. Was there ever a time, I wondered, when the apostle Paul looked up from his travels and said, "Lord, I can't do this. I'm not man enough. I'm not strong enough." But then, perhaps I am putting onto the apostle the shortcomings of my own faith, and that is not a fair comparison.

I wanted to become a writer. I was always talking about my novel in progress. I don't think anyone in Eden Springs realized that there really was no book—except in my imagination. But I could see it there, its hardbound pages fluttering just in front of me as I strolled the old sidewalks of the town square, or drove along the river in my Isuzu Trooper. To me, the book was as real as if it had already been published and sat on my shelf at home, wedged between the dogeared volumes of F. Scott Fitzgerald and Robert Frost.

Each night I sat at my makeshift desk in my little apartment and tried to write. It was an exasperating experience. I came to hate the number "1" because each time that heading appeared on the screen of my computer, it was like a death knell—killing off my exuberant dreams and imagination—or like a tedious obligation I was not capable of fulfilling.

For example, one evening I typed:

Bonner, the hired man, came across the field like he was being chased by a rabid dog. The pant legs of his overalls dragged in the dust and kicked up little puffs with each stride as he climbed the rise though the yellow sunflowers to where I was mending the fence. Each year it seemed those cows got out through the same hole.

"Matt!" he gasped. "You better come quick!"

So before the last words wheezed out of his gaping mouth, I was down off the fence, dropping my hammer, and legging it back to the house as fast as I could in those heavy work boots.

Ma was standing in the doorway as I came up to the porch, and I could not for the life of me figure out what was wrong. Naturally, at first I thought someone had died, or had been hurt badly in an accident. Maybe Ma had suffered another stroke, and my stomach seemed to drop to my knees when I saw Bonner running and he said I'd better come quick. On the prairie you never know what is going to happen and when it does, you always expect the worst.

So I was nervous when I reached the plank porch and saw Ma standing there. She was wringing her hands in the old apron she always wore tied around her waist—even when she wasn't cooking. Then Della came from inside the house. Her face looked strained and worried, like she was trying hard to work something out, but it wouldn't come.

The first thing I had thought of was Ma being sick, so when I saw her standing there, even nervous and fidgeting as she was, it was a great relief. Yet, I couldn't figure out what had happened, and surely something had gone wrong for them to send Bonner running out into the fields after me. I turned my gaze from one woman to the other, and though Ma seemed the most disturbed by whatever had transpired, it was Della's eyes that read danger behind the brown, fixed gaze.

"What is it?" I asked breathlessly, scared to know.

"It's Liz, Matt," Della said finally. "You'd better get the truck."

I hurried back to the shed and within another few minutes we were on the road, racing past the old homesteads and sand hills to *town. I was worried, but more than that, I was confused as Della cradled Liz in her arms. Liz looked pale, crying sometimes and looking wide-eyed and scared like a frightened mare. And Della saying, "Now, don't worry, Liz. We'll get you there. You just keep calm like I told you." And then adding, "Maybe you could say a prayer. That always helps me."*

And then Liz clouding up like a stormfront moving in fast from the west, so that you could see the clouds racing across the prairie in dark waves.

Sitting at my desk in the late hours of the evening, I gazed at my computer screen and thought I had written a pretty good opening. I would go on to tell about Liz and why she was staying with the Porters, how Matt felt about her, how hard their life was on the prairie, and why Matt had been sent to get the truck. It was a long, complicated story.

"Okay," I told myself. "Maybe this time it will go all the way."

But as the days dragged on and the pages slowly accumulated, I came to a disappointing realization: I didn't know enough about this family and their difficult circumstances to write about them. So, with reluctance, I set the story aside. I say this in a metaphorical sense, for in reality, I simply moved it from one computer folder to another. I would get back to it someday, I told myself. The Porters and Liz would always be there, waiting for me, when I knew the rest of their story.

As with everyone else in the United States, the residents of Eden Springs had watched the sudden bursts of light in the night sky over Baghdad on their televisions that January, and had listened to the excited voices of the news commentators when the Gulf War began. The beginning of the war was something too vast and significant to really believe. I remember driving across town and listening to the radio as a DJ played tunes that were popular in the Vietnam War. These were for our boys in the Middle East, he said. Could it possibly be, I thought, that we were beginning another Vietnam?

Fortunately we were not, and within a few months I received word that Tag was coming home on leave. "Received word" is a little presumptuous here. Actually I ran into his mother at Hazel's cafe.

"Richard's coming home," she informed me brightly, with the enthusiasm only a mother could produce.

"Maybe we can do a feature on him for the paper," I suggested.

"I don't know," she said thoughtfully. "He's had a hard time. I don't know if he would want any publicity."

"Why?" I asked. "What happened?"

But she had paid for her lunch and was walking out the door. The little bell above the door rang as she stepped out to the sidewalk.

"I'll have him give you a call, Donny," she said.

The call came through two weeks later as I was working on a story about a proposal by the City Council Public Works Committee to expand Cottonwood Road and to improve River Trail Park. I had spent the morning interviewing the director of municipal services and the park superintendent.

"Hello, Donny," the voice said.

It took me a moment to adjust my thoughts. Even the dullest story requires concentration—perhaps even more concentration.

"Yes," I replied.

"It's Tag," he said. "I'm back in town."

His voice was immediately familiar and yet different somehow, as if the texture had changed, settled, become more reserved.

We talked for a minute, but I could perceive a tenseness over the line, as if he didn't really want to discuss anything on the telephone.

"I'll come over after work," I offered.

"See you then," he said and immediately hung up.

Well, I thought, he has been in the service for three years, and in a war. That would change anyone.

It was early June, and the Midwest was expanding and ripening into that soft, green vastness of fields and budding trees and flowers which I always enjoyed. I opened the sunroof of my old Trooper as I drove and listened to a jet making its approach to the base. We were only two miles from the base perimeter, so jets were always taking off or coming in for landings over the town. Through my windshield, I could see an F15 banking sharply. It passed to the north of town and then turned to the west. A moment later a second F15, the wing man, began the same approach. They would be flying a lot now that the weather was so clear.

I turned up Thirty-fifth Street and made a left on Gardner. When I pulled up in front of Tag's house, I had to stop for a moment and look. I had spent a lot of good times in this house, and in some ways it was a part of my youth, just as it was for Tag. The thing I remembered most was the windows. The Taggarts enjoyed brightly lit rooms, and there were ten windows (if you counted the high attic window) on the street side alone. Each window was accented with green shutters that stood out dramatically against the white frame of the house. There was a large front porch with four round wooden pillars, and steps leading down to the walk. The elm tree we had climbed so often as boys had been trimmed, and the lower, more accessible branches had been removed. Even though Tag's father had been dead for eight years now, the house still looked well maintained.

Tag met me at the door and invited me inside. He looked a little pale—he had just returned from a VA hospital. But the ruggedness was still there, and that inestimable quality of energy.

"I brought something for you, Donny," he said and disappeared into a back room. When he came out again, he was carrying something wrapped in a piece of cloth.

"Here," he said, handing the parcel to me. "I remember how you always liked this kind of stuff when we were kids."

I unwrapped the cloth and held up a bayonet in a scabbard.

"It's Iraqi," he explained. "Made in Baghdad."

"Thanks," I said and gazed at him closely.

A quick smile came to his mouth, hesitated for a moment, and then disappeared. As it vanished, I perceived some undefinable sadness about him, as if the misfortunes of our past are never so far away as we might believe.

"So what now?" he asked expectantly.

Perhaps it was my imagination, but I sensed a slight undercurrent of desperation in his voice.

"There's a dance at the Rotary Club," I suggested. "I thought we could get something to eat and then drive over to the dance."

I could hear his mother putting away dishes in the kitchen —a practical excuse for listening in on our conversation.

"Okay," he said, running a hand over his short dark hair. "Let me run upstairs and change my shirt."

When he came down again, he was wearing a loose-fitting white cotton shirt and jeans.

"Let's hit it," he said, and I had just enough time to grab my car keys before he was out the door. I caught a glimpse of his mother leaning out from the kitchen. She seemed to hold a question in her gaze, as if she wanted to say all the motherly things, but realized that her son was a returned war veteran now and not the little boy I had played *Wiffle ball* with in the driveway so many years ago. Or was it that she was worried about something of which I was unaware? At that moment I had no way to tell.

"Nice to see you again, Mrs. Taggart," I called.

"Come by anytime, Donny," she said.

On our way downtown to the Sonic, Tag asked me to pull over at a Quick Trip, and he ran inside to buy a six-pack of beer.

"Got to have a little cold brew," he explained.

When we reached the Sonic, I pulled up to one of the slots and ordered two cheeseburgers and fries. Tag ripped a can of beer from the six-pack and offered it to me.

"No thanks."

"Still mister squeaky-clean, eh, Donny?"

"Not so much anymore, Tag," I said. "It's more of a promise I made to myself a long time ago."

"You can't live in the past, old buddy," he advised. "Doesn't work."

"I try not to," I said sincerely.

Tag gazed fondly around the Sonic. "But those were good times, eh, Donny?" he sighed. "We were running mates then, weren't we?"

"That's right."

"Too bad it's all gone now."

"What do you mean?"

"Lost," he said, as if this answer would provide more clarity. "I mean, this town used to be the big pond and we were the king frogs. And now," he hesitated and closed his eyes. "Now I can barely stand it."

"You've been in a war," I said. "What could be the same after that?"

"Nothing," he said and shook his head wearily. "Nothing at all."

The Rotary Club was a mile beyond the city limits on Route 9. As we left the houses behind and rolled out into the twilight fields, we could see the sun glowing pale yellow on the wheat. The farmers would be harvesting soon. Tag lifted his hands into the air through the sunroof.

"I remember doing this in Riyadh," he said, his raised arms blowing in the warm darkness. "We were in a Jeep on the road to the airbase."

"Did you like it?" I asked.

"Like it?" he responded, as if he had never thought of this question before. "You survive it, Donny, and then you remember it. That's all."

"Can you tell me about it?"

He pulled his arms down. "As a friend, or as a reporter?"

So his mother had spoken to him about my suggestion, I thought. Or perhaps he was just thinking of my occupation.

"As a friend, of course."

He gazed ahead at the two-lane blacktop caught in our headlights. "I'll tell you sometime, Donny," he said seriously. "But not tonight. Okay?"

"Sure."

Two

A head we could see a string of yellow party lights hanging in front of the Rotary Club. A Bruce Springsteen tune drifted out to the gravel parking lot. I rolled my Trooper into a parking space and shut off the motor. Tag looked suddenly nervous.

"Something wrong?" I asked.

"Think there'll be many kids from the old days?" he asked.

"A few, probably. Not so many anymore."

"Okay," he said with determination. "Let's go."

The dance floor was crowded with couples dancing to rock music. On the far side were tables with red tablecloths and candles. There were more people than I had expected, and we had to edge our way over to the makeshift bar. This was a long table with two punch bowls at one end and a bartender at the other.

"Drink?" I asked Tag.

"Yeah," he said, gazing around the room.

"A beer and a club soda," I told the bartender.

"Good heavens, it's Tag," I heard a female voice shout above the music, and I turned with the drinks in my hands to see a brunette hugging Tag. When she pulled back, I could see it was Shirley Cormack. She had been in our class, gotten married shortly after graduation, and divorced a year later. Now she was going with a dentist from Springfield.

Tag nodded self-consciously.

"How long have you been back?" she asked. "I heard you were in the war."

"Not too long," Tag muttered and took the beer I offered him.

"You'll just have to come over some time," Shirley said. "I imagine you have so many stories to tell."

"Not really."

She looked back at her date and then gave Tag's arm a pinch. "You call me, now, okay?"

"Sure," Tag said.

Shirley moved off toward the dance floor.

I looked at Tag. His face was taut, and his hand trembled a little as he raised the beer to his mouth.

"This is harder than I expected," he said.

We found a vacant table and sat down. The music was too loud to carry on any kind of serious conversation, so we watched the dancers moving around the floor. Tag pulled a cigarette lighter from his pocket and moved it absently through the fingers of his right hand. The lighter had an Air Force emblem on the side.

"I didn't know you smoked," I commented.

"Oh, this," he said, gazing at the lighter. "I don't. It belonged to an airman buddy of mine in the Gulf. He was..."

I waited for Tag to continue, but he had stopped talking and was looking blankly at the dance floor.

"He was what?" I asked.

Tag glanced at me as if I had asked about something classified.

"Nothing," he answered.

He looked around the club with an attitude of boredom, and I began to feel sorry I had gotten him into this. I was just leaning forward to suggest we leave when

I saw a young woman with curly red hair coming toward us. It was my cousin Melissa.

"Donny," she said, giving me a hug. "I didn't know you were coming tonight."

"We're just out cruising."

"Where's Anne?"

"She doesn't get off work till eleven."

Melissa looked at Tag.

"This is Richard Taggart," I said, introducing them. "Melissa is my cousin—on the Graham side of the family."

Tag stood up and held out his hand. "We've met before, but it has been a long time," he said.

Melissa gazed at him thoughtfully and then smiled. "Oh, yes. You're the boy my father used to see climbing up the wisteria vine to your room at dawn. You had been out all night."

Tag smiled. "I did that a few times."

"Did your parents ever find out?"

"Not yet," he said.

"Tag is on leave from the Air Force," I explained.

"I thought so," Melissa said. "He's got the look."

"What look?" Tag asked suspiciously.

"The haircut," Melissa said and laughed. "Would you like to join us? We have a table over there."

I glanced at Tag, and he nodded.

"Fine," I said.

We picked up our drinks and moved over to the table. Another young woman was sitting there, tapping her fingers to the music. I could tell from the back of her head that it was Sylvie, Melissa's younger sister. She had always been one of my favorite cousins. She was three years younger and had such an angelic expression that I always thought of her as a saint. Her hair was cut short and brushed back away from her face, exposing the pale curve of her neck. She looked up at me with sensitive eyes the color of dark honey and smiled pleasantly. Sylvie had the most expressive mouth I had ever known on a young woman. Putting a hand up to the back of her neck, she glanced at Tag.

Well, I thought as I made the introductions, Tag still had the touch with females. As we sat down, the DJ put on "I Got You" by James Brown. Tag asked Sylvie if she would like to dance. I was surprised because he had seemed so bored and hesitant at first. They moved out on the dance floor, and Melissa and I watched them for a moment. Sylvie danced shyly but with good rhythm. Tag, on the other hand, was barely moving. But it was obvious that he felt the music. His expression was almost blank, eyes half-closed. I wondered what he was thinking. I remembered him in high school, the football letter jacket, the easy, confident grin. So much of our youthful confidence was based on ignorance, I thought. We stepped into life so aggressively, with so much belief in ourselves. But that soon vanished when we realized how very small and inconsequential we actually were. Perhaps Tag had discovered that in Saudi Arabia. But it didn't take a war to teach that lesson. He must have gone through much worse and come to decisions far greater than anything I had known. In a way, I envied him his experience. I knew it was something I would never be able to completely understand.

"So what's wrong with Tag?" Melissa asked.

"What do you mean?"

"Come on, Donny," she said. "I know you well enough to read your expressions. I can tell you're worried about this guy."

I took a swig of club soda. "He's just back from the Gulf. He seems really nervous, and I know something is bothering him."

"Going over there would make anyone nervous."

"I hope that's all it is."

"What else could it be?" she asked.

Before I could answer, the music stopped and Tag and Sylvie came off the dance floor.

Sylvie slipped into her chair and smiled at me. Her cheeks were flushed, and the strands of hair around the edges of her face were damp.

"It gets warm quickly," she said, fanning herself with a napkin.

"Would you like something to drink?" Tag asked. He was being courteous now.

"A Sprite," she said.

Tag looked at Melissa.

"Me too."

Tag went off to get the drinks.

"Having fun?" I asked Sylvie stupidly.

She smiled. "So your friend is in the Air Force?"

I nodded. The music had started again.

"In the Gulf War?"

I nodded again.

She tilted her head thoughtfully and gazed across the room. It was getting really crowded now.

Tag came back with the drinks.

"One more time?" he asked Sylvie, motioning to the dancers.

She rubbed a hand across her damp hair and shrugged at me. "Maybe just once."

"This is getting old," Melissa said as we watched them moving toward the floor. "Let's dance too."

So we joined them.

On the drive back to his house, Tag was quiet and sat hunched down in the seat.

"Tell me about Sylvie," he said finally. "Is she involved with anybody—you know, serious?"

"Not anymore," I answered, and I realized that even the saints among us had so much baggage.

Tag nodded.

"Would you mind," he asked, gazing out the window at the fields passing in the darkness, "If I asked her out? You know, just to get something to eat or go bowling or something?"

"Of course not."

He seemed to cheer up a little at this and flicked on the car radio. An old song by Crosby, Stills & Nash sounded through the front speakers.

"It's getting to the point, where I'm no fun anymore, I am sorry. . ."

"Pull over," Tag said.

"What?"

"Pull over."

I pulled the Trooper onto the gravel shoulder of the road. On either side of the car were dark woods. Behind us I could see other cars coming from the club.

"What's up?" I asked.

"I need to get out and walk a bit," Tag said. "Just for a while. I can't explain it."

"What do you want me to do?"

He looked up the road to where the taillights of a car were just disappearing over the top of a hill.

"Drive up the road about a half-mile and wait for me. I won't be very long."

He climbed out and stood beside the car. A white Chevy honked as it passed, and I heard the receding voice of Shirley Cormack calling to us.

"Wait a minute," Tag said. He reached into the back seat and took the last can of beer.

"Okay, Donny," he said. "Thanks."

I pulled away slowly and then gazed at the odometer. The numerals glowed green in the darkness. When I reached a half-mile, I pulled into the parking area of a gas station that was closed for the night and shut off the engine. Above my head I could see Orion, and I tried to name the other constellations, but I was never any good at that. It was a pleasant early summer night, and after a moment of irritation at Tag for pulling such a stunt, I began to appreciate the peaceful quiet of the countryside. Was this what he had needed? I wondered. To get away from everything and make this quiet walk before going home? From time to time a car passed. I could hear the cars coming from a long way up the road. Finally I saw his white shirt faintly in the darkness and watched as he approached.

"Ready?" I asked.

"Yeah," he said calmly.

Tag climbed into the passenger seat once again, and I sped off. It was almost midnight now, and I had not seen another car on the road for several minutes. Tag slumped in the seat and was nodding his head slowly, as if listening to music through invisible headphones. I felt awkward and did not say anything. Was I supposed to crack a joke? I wondered. Get serious? Ignore him? What? I didn't know. So I drove until we hit Thirty-fifth Street and the pale street lights flickered over our heads.

When we came to a stop in front of Tag's house, he just sat there for a moment. At first I thought maybe he had fallen asleep. His mother had left the front porch lights on—one on either side of the large front door—and they burned yellow in the darkness.

"Well," I said awkwardly. "We're back."

Tag seemed to come out of his trance.

"Right," he muttered wearily and reached for the door handle. "See you tomorrow, Donny."

"I'll give you a call," I said.

Tag leaned against the window frame and looked at

me questioningly. "We were running pals, weren't we, Donny?" he asked.

"We still *are*," I said emphatically.

He nodded thoughtfully. "And it's okay about Sylvie?"

"She's a nice girl, Tag," I said, beginning to have second thoughts. "And she's my cousin . . ."

He thumped the top of the Trooper. "Direct hit," he said and I got the impression that perhaps he wasn't talking to me.

I watched him walk up to the porch, fumble with his keys and go inside. Then I drove slowly up Gardner Avenue. Passing the dark houses, I felt suddenly guilty, as if there was something I should have done or said to change Tag's mood. I always felt this tremendous sense of responsibility toward my close friends, and who was closer to me than Tag? No one except Anne, and I knew that I would give her a call as soon as I got home. She would still be up, and I wanted to hear her voice. Maybe if she wasn't too tired . . .

Then I thought about Tag again. With some people you can tell within a fair approximation how life will change them, mold them into the person they were meant to be. You can look at them and think, Yes, this is how I thought you would turn out all along. But what happens when some unforeseen event comes along and changes everything? War had never been in the game plan for any of us. Had it affected Joshua so long ago, or David? Would they have been different, thought in different ways, struggled with different torments in their tents at night, if they had not experienced war? No doubt, I thought. But wasn't that for the best? Didn't God always send us what we needed to prepare ourselves for this life?

I had an apartment on the town square above a row of small shops. My apartment was directly above Cleary's

Watch Shop, and I saw that the metal shutters of the shop had been lowered when I pulled into a curbside parking space. It had been a long day, and I felt tired. Had it been only this morning, I mused, that I had been working on that tedious public works story? Yes, and now I wished I had put more into it. Well, maybe I could do a follow-up later in the week. A young couple came out of a cafe down the street and passed me. The girl was laughing at something the young man had said. He was smiling appreciatively. Then I heard someone call my name.

"You're lucky," Anne said. "I was only going to give you five more minutes."

"Yes," I said, pulling her close to me and smelling the warm summer night in her hair. But I knew there was no such thing as luck in a world where we were given what we needed—even if we could not see it at the time. And if only I had listened to myself at that moment, what a lot of trouble I could have been spared.

Three

~

I didn't see Tag for a week after the Rotary Club dance. Perhaps this was coincidental, or perhaps there was some underlying hesitancy on my part. I had intended to call him the next day, but an assignment came up at the newspaper which kept me busy. Then, when I did phone, he was out. I wondered if his mother knew about his drinking. If she did, I wondered if she ignored the problem or if it was a source of tension between them. Perhaps that was why her face had been touched with worry when I dropped by to pick him up that evening. She must have known Tag was trying to work things out, to sort through the experience of being in a war and to come up with something positive. I didn't know, and it wasn't my place to ask.

I did hear from Melissa, however. She phoned a few days later and said that Tag had asked Sylvie out for a pizza.

"Maybe she'll be good for him," I suggested, recalling how eager he had been to seek my approval.

"What are we doing here?" Melissa asked tersely. "Sacrificing my sister for the benefit of a guy who needs help?"

"Not at all," I said. "They only went out for a pizza. Give him a break."

"But he asked her out again tonight, Donny. If Sylvie gets hurt in any way, I'm holding you responsible."

"Okay," I said. "I'll talk to him."

"No," she said flatly. "I don't want you to talk to *him*. I want you to talk to *her*."

I was beginning to understand now. "Does she still get off work at the preschool at noon?"

"Yes," Melissa answered.

"Then I'll stop by and see if she wants to have lunch. Okay?"

"Okay," Melissa said and hesitated.

I knew what was coming next.

"You know, Donny," she said after a moment. "Sylvie isn't like us. She's one of the innocents."

"Can you still talk that way?" I asked. "After. . ."

"Yes," she said adamantly, interrupting me. "I can, and I always will."

"All right," I said. I had already learned that some people never got over the loss of innocence—in themselves or others. It was like someone pulling off their rose-colored glasses and stepping on them, or like being tossed out of the garden. It was a difficult perspective to lose. So for some, the next best thing to being in the garden itself was to *pretend* to be in the garden. It was a mental outlook that had its advantages, but it certainly did complicate things.

"I think that's why Tag likes her," I offered.

"Of course," Melissa said. "Just keep an eye on him. Okay?"

"I will," I promised, meaning it and wishing it could have always been true.

So at half past eleven, I walked up the long sloping hill to Gage Street and the Eden Springs Preschool. Sylvie was working there to help pay for her classes in elementary education at the college in Warrenton. I knew she would be an excellent teacher because she had the gift of infinite patience. When I reached the gate, I could see children piling excitedly into vans and cars for their trips home. Sylvie was not outside, so I walked in through the front door and veered right to her classroom. She was wiping off table tops with a damp rag. When she looked up, I could tell that for a moment she had thought I was Tag. But there was no sign of disappointment on her face.

"Donny," she said and smiled sweetly. "What brings you here?"

"I thought maybe we could have lunch together."

She gazed at me steadily with those beautiful honeyed eyes. "Have you been talking with Melissa?"

I thought about lying for a moment, but decided to tell the truth. Anyway, I was never very good at lying.

"She called me this morning."

"And she wants you to talk to me, right?"

I shrugged. "I wanted to see you anyway. It's been too long."

"Well," she glanced around the classroom. "I guess I'm finished here. Did you bring your Trooper?"

"No. I walked over."

"And you probably want to go to Hazel's?"

"They have the fried chicken special today," I suggested with enthusiasm.

Sylvie grimaced. "I suppose I could get a salad."

We walked down the sidewalk in the warm June sunshine past the bank and the book shop. Sylvie walked with her hands clasped behind her back. She had put on a large, white summer hat.

"So," she began. "You might as well tell me about him."

"He's intense," I said. "Always has been."

"That's obvious," she commented. "Melissa says our dad used to see him coming home at dawn. What do you think he was doing?"

"I don't know anything about that," I said. "But I know he's led a fast life."

Sylvie brushed a strand of hair behind her ear. "He's so funny," she said, her eyes shining amusedly. "I just laughed and laughed."

"I'm glad you had a good time."

We reached Hazel's cafe. There were no open tables because of the lunch crowd, so we sat on stools at the counter.

"We're going out again tonight," Sylvie offered, as she glanced at the menu. "But then, you probably already know that."

"Yes," I admitted.

"Tag seems to miss doing everyday, ordinary things so much."

It was as if she had sensed through some sort of unspoken female empathy the nature of Tag's grief and had determined a plan to set him straight again.

"He drinks," I said abruptly.

She nodded and took a sip of water thoughtfully. "He told me about that. He says it keeps away a terrible panic that comes over him sometimes. I think if he can get rid of that feeling, he'll stop."

"Maybe," I said.

A waitress hurried up to us and hesitated long enough to take our order. Then she sped away.

"I don't know why you like this place so much, Donny," Sylvie said, looking around the cafe. "It's always so crowded."

I had to smile. "Because of Grandpa," I said. "He used to bring me here almost every Saturday morning for breakfast. Don't you remember?"

Sylvie shook her head. "Grandpa Graham?"

I nodded.

The waitress returned and slid a plate of fried chicken with mashed potatoes and green beans in front of me. She gave Sylvie a lunch salad with iceburg lettuce and sliced tomatoes.

"Iced tea?" she asked us.

We both nodded, and she sped away again.

"So where was I while you were having lunch or breakfast or whatever with Grandpa?" Sylvie asked, continuing our conversation.

"I don't know," I said. "With Grandmother, I suppose. She was always teaching you how to make quilts."

Sylvie poured Italian dressing on her salad. "It's so funny how each of us has a different perspective on our childhood."

"In the small details," I said. "But not the big ones."

"No," she agreed, smiling. "Not the big ones. We had wonderful grandparents, didn't we?"

I nodded and spread butter on my roll. Hazel's rolls were the best thing about the cafe and another reason why I ate lunch there almost every day.

"Is there anything else you want to tell me about Tag?" Sylvie asked.

"He's not saved," I said and felt immediately ashamed. It wasn't my place to decide who was saved or not. Nor did I have any inclination as to what was going on in Tag's heart concerning God.

"You know that for a fact?" Sylvie asked.

"No, I don't," I replied. "And I'm sorry I mentioned it."

"So he might be?"

I took a bite of green beans. "Tag has changed a lot since he came back from the Gulf, and I have no idea what he thinks about things now," I explained. "I only know that before he left he didn't believe."

Sylvie did not reply but gazed at the counter thoughtfully. I felt a sudden distance between us.

"Listen," I said contritely. "Melissa just wants you to be careful, that's all. She doesn't want you to get hurt."

"I won't, Donny," Sylvie said and patted my hand. "Don't worry."

Four

~

When you begin to spend time again with an old friend, it puts you in a curious predicament, because it is a relationship built in the past and existing in the past. You find yourself inevitably talking about and laughing over incidents that occurred in a previous time, and you see each other as you saw each other then. For a short time this can be pleasant, even necessary—especially if you liked who you were then—but eventually it becomes monotonous because both of you have changed. I have always believed that the spirit remains young as the body ages, but that doesn't mean there is no change, that we aren't altered by the situations we experience. I was far from the teenager who had played Wiffle ball with Tag in his driveway, and it was obvious that he had traveled just as far, and probably much farther. So I was determined that my friendship with him would move into the present. To do that, I needed to find out who he was now. That might sound easy enough, but as I said before, with Tag you never knew where you stood.

On Sunday I half expected to see him arrive at church with Sylvie. It would not be the first time, I thought, that a young man had inadvertently found God while escorting a young woman to a service. But as I moved from aisle to aisle with the offering plate, (our pastor had volunteered me for a variety of jobs) I saw Melissa and Sylvie sitting by themselves. The First Assembly Church of Eden Springs had not yet made another convert.

After church I dropped Anne off at her home and drove past Tag's house. He was sitting in one of the green rocking chairs on his front porch.

"Hey, Donny," he called. "I just tried to phone you."

"I was over at Anne's," I explained. "What are you doing?"

"Nothing . . . nothing worth talking about anyway."

"Want to shoot some skeet?"

"Sounds great!" he said.

I had thought about driving out to the bluff overlooking the strip mine, but I knew Tag would want to take a six-pack with us and I didn't want to encourage that. I had also thought about the river. There was an embankment just west of the trellis bridge where we had taken dates when we were younger, but that area would be filled with poison ivy and mosquitoes this time of the year. Anyway, I wasn't in the mood to skip stones or watch passing trains. I was in the mood for something competitive, to feel the kick of a gun butt against my shoulder, to show Tag that this small-town boy could still take him in clay pigeons—no matter where he had been.

The skeet club was southwest of town near the wildlife reserve. It had actually been founded by pilots from the base, but anyone could shoot without being a member. When we pulled up, I saw several Toyota pickup trucks with small camper backs parked near the clubhouse. For some reason, this seemed to be the vehicle of preference for Air Force pilots. I assumed it had something to do with status. Was it because they needed to stow flight gear in the back? I could have simply asked one of them—several went to our church—but that would have been a slight to my reporting skills. No, I would figure it out deductively in time.

We went into the clubhouse to register and to rent a gun for Tag. I had brought along the 20-gauge pump my grandfather had given me on my sixteenth birthday. It wasn't the best shotgun in the world for shooting skeet— the barrel was a little long—but it had been my grandfather's, and so I kept it.

Many of the pilots stationed at Emerson had been in England, and at some point in time, one of them had nailed up a dartboard on the clubhouse wall. This activity had become almost as popular with the club members as shooting skeet. Three pilots were playing a game of darts now. I recognized one of them.

"Hello, Mark," I said. "Winning?"

Captain Mark Wayland pulled a dart from the board and looked at me. He was a slender young man with an intense gaze—the stereotypical jet driver. They all seemed to fit a certain body type, which I assumed was because they had to squeeze into those narrow fighter cockpits. All the pilots I had known fit this description.

"Want to play a game, Donny?" Wayland asked.

I had played against him several times, and he was always a good sport, though extremely competitive.

"Thanks," I said, "but we're here to shoot."

"Come on, Wayland," one of the other pilots called.

I watched their game for a moment while Tag checked out a gun. Wayland threw a dart, and it missed the bull's-eye by a quarter of an inch.

"You throw that thing like a Scud missile," the third pilot sneered derisively. "Let me show you how it's done."

They all laughed.

Tag had come up behind me.

"Are you okay?" I asked.

He wiped his forehead on the sleeve of his shirt.

"I just need some air," he said. "It's too hot in here."

We walked outside into the hot afternoon and down the path to one of the shooting stations. We were at no. 8.

"You go first," Tag urged.

"Okay," I said, taking my firing stance. I swayed the gun from left to right several times to get my rhythm, then slipped the safety off.

"Ready?" Tag asked.

"Pull," I said.

The clay pigeon shot off to my right like a miniature UFO. I swung sharply, a bit too sharply, and squeezed on the trigger. The gun slammed into my shoulder. My shot only nicked the back end of the disk.

"I was a bit off on that one," I said, not turning around. "I'll try again."

There was no response from Tag.

I resumed my firing stance.

"Pull," I said.

A second pigeon flew through the air, and this time I got the lead right and my shot hit it about fifty yards out.

"That's better," I said, flicking the safety back on. "I don't know why . . ."

I had turned around and was looking at Tag. He was just standing there, gazing at the ground, his right hand wrapped tightly around his upper left arm. He looked as if he were desperately trying to hold on to himself.

"Tag?" I asked, concerned. "What's the matter?"

His breath was coming in shallow gasps.

"I think I need to get home, Donny," he said. "I'm not feeling so well."

"Can you make it to the car?" I asked.

He nodded. "If you'll check in the gun . . ."

"Of course," I said.

Tag went out to the Trooper while I checked in his shotgun. Then I drove back to his house as quickly as possible. What was going on here? I asked myself. In the clubhouse he had seemed to be nervous about something. Then outside he had started to hyperventilate. Was there a serious problem that he hadn't shared with me? There must be—I had never seen him act this way before. Glancing over at him now, I saw that he was slumped down in the seat with his eyes closed. He still looked distressed, but the color had returned to his face.

"Tag?" I asked. "Are you all right?"

He took a deep breath and exhaled slowly without opening his eyes. "Yes," he said. "I'm all right."

"I mean, really?"

"It's just that sometimes . . ." he began and then paused. "Sometimes . . ."

But he did not complete the phrase. Instead his voice drifted off, and he gazed out the window at the passing fields. What was he seeing? I wondered as I watched him. Was it the sand dunes of Saudi Arabia out there, an airfield with jets coming in for landings on a cold desert morning, or was it that deep tranquility one felt when gazing at the countryside after a long absence? I knew for myself that each time I drove out to the country—out into the fields—it was as if the tension of the day fell off me, a tension of which I had not even been aware. Perhaps it was that way for Tag also. He was just tired, I told myself, trying to rationalize his behavior, to put it into a more comfortable framework. He was just tired, and I had been stupid to suggest that we shoot skeet. But that was the problem. I had not been around him enough recently to know where his boundaries lay. How was I to know what would affect him? I didn't, and it was beginning to frustrate and anger me.

"Listen," I said when we reached his house. "You've got to level with me. If there is a problem . . . I can't go around wondering all the time if something is going to bother you."

He seemed to have recovered almost completely now and shook his head despondently. "I know," he said. "It isn't fair."

"Can I do anything?"

"No. It's just going to take some time, that's all."

"For what?"

He gave a short, dry laugh. "For life to move on. For me to find some . . . some . . ."

Again he let his thoughts drift. It was as if he had suddenly turned his gaze inward and was surveying the internal damage, adding up the possibilities, trying to gauge in some realistic way the amount of time it would take to rebuild what had been lost.

"Some what?" I asked after a moment.

"Huh?"

"You said you were looking for something. Something about life moving on."

"I don't know," he said, suddenly himself again. "Right now, all I want is a beer and to call Sylvie. Want to come in?"

"Thanks, but I have to get going."

"I'm really sorry about the skeet shooting," he said. "Maybe some other time. Okay?"

"Sure," I said, knowing that it would never happen. Another square from the old days had been checked off. Would there be new squares, I wondered, new additions to this friendship? Or would we keep on checking off squares until it became apparent one day that we no longer had anything in common?

"And about Sylvie . . ." I added.

"What?" he asked and gazed at me with that familiar intensity. Whatever had come over him was gone now.

"I don't have to tell you," I said.

We were still close enough friends for that kind of understanding.

"Right," Tag said. "You can trust me."

"I know," I replied, and I watched him go slowly up the sidewalk.

Five

~

ag reported back to duty at Emerson after his second week of leave. I had not seen him in his uniform since his departure for the Gulf, so it was a shock to see him again in his BDUs. But then, they seemed to fit him in a way that civilian clothes never had—so that something of the inner man was revealed—and I felt as if I were really looking at him for the first time. I realized that he was a man with serious responsibilities and experience. In rank he was a senior airman and assistant crew chief on one of the many F16s that flew out of Emerson. I didn't know that much about the technical work of the ground crews, but I did know that as an assistant crew chief, Tag was responsible for maintenance on his jet.

And, of course, he was still seeing Sylvie. I wondered if she liked him in his uniform. In some ways, I had expected their relationship to play out quickly—they seemed to be so different from each other. But rather than diminishing, it seemed as if a bond had developed between them, something that could not be seen but that could be perceived, just as you are aware of an unspoken understanding between members of a church, or among conspirators.

I was thinking about Tag and Sylvie one morning at the newspaper when the managing editor, Ed Thomas, came up to me. He was a tall, muscular man with a sharp nose and a balding head. He had been a halfback in high school and still carried himself as if he were wearing shoulder pads.

"What are you working on?" he asked bruskly.

I leaned back from my computer and stretched. I had turned my desk so that I could see the street, giving me a beautiful view of the parking meters, several parked cars, and a few trees near the hardware store.

"A report on site drainage improvements in Eden Springs," I said. "This is Pulitzer stuff."

"The Cottonwood Road proposal?"

"That's it."

"Then you should take this call. Deputy Sheriff Hastings is on line two."

"Thanks."

"Brief me on it when you're finished."

"All right," I said.

Thomas walked across the newsroom toward his office.

I picked up the receiver and pushed line two. Jim Hastings was an old friend.

"Jim, this is Donny," I said, grabbing my notepad and pencil. "What's up?"

"We've got a situation over here I thought might interest you," Jim replied.

"Fine," I said. "I'm bored stiff with this Cottonwood Road proposal story."

"Sorry, but this ties in with it."

"What is it?" I asked wearily.

Jim explained that a secretary in the City Works Department had just been implicated in a scam on the proposal bids. Two construction companies—Kaplan from Eden Springs and Copely from the city—had submitted proposals for the expansion and drainage work. The secretary was accused of leaking the proposal figures to a third company, Braynard Construction, which had then submitted a bid just below those of the other two.

"You mean she tried to undercut the bids?" I asked.

"Right," Jim said.

"What's her name?"

"Let's see."

I could hear him shuffling through his papers.

"Mary Leighton," he said.

"You're kidding?"

"Do you know her?"

"She goes to our church. She has three kids."

"Some federal funds are involved, so this makes it a federal offense in either fraud or racketeering," Jim continued. "If found guilty, she could get prison time. I don't expect that, but she will certainly lose her job."

"It seems impossible," I said, astounded. "Is this the same Mary Leighton who lives on Mayfair Road? Her husband, Jeff, sells farm equipment?"

"That's correct," Jim said.

"Who found out about it?"

"Her boss overheard her making the call."

"Do you think she would really be that careless?"

"I guess she didn't realize he was listening. You'll have to ask her about that yourself."

"I will," I said. "Who's her boss?"

"His name is Stan Drussell."

"Where is Mary now?"

"We brought her in for questioning this morning. We also brought in the manager of Braynard Construction. A warrant is being issued. I imagine she'll be home by this afternoon."

"Did she confess to making the call?" I asked.

"No," Jim said.

As I hung up the telephone, a sadness came over me. I had hoped our little community of Eden Springs would be devoid of corruption. That was foolish, I knew. I had always thought of it as a place where evil flowed around us but never through us. It was not saintly nor holy nor sanctified in any way—any more than any other small town—but I had always felt a special quality about Eden Springs that I had perceived nowhere else. But there again, that was my perception of life here and my interpretation of the truth. The truth was that there was corruption everywhere and that no city or town or home was immune to its conflagration.

"So, what have you got?" the managing editor asked as I entered his office.

I told him about Mary Leighton and Braynard Construction and the possible bidding scam.

"The sheriff's office has requested a court order to check the telephone records," I added.

Ed Thomas nodded and tapped a pencil thoughtfully against his knee. "I hope it isn't true," he sighed. "You'd like to think . . ."

"I know," I said.

He glanced out the window. "What's the financial proposal on this project?"

I leaned forward and checked my notes. "The Public Works Committee is asking for $1.8 million."

The managing editor blew softly through his teeth. "That's a lot of money."

"Well, they're planning a lot of work."

Thomas swiveled in his chair and gazed at the wall clock. "It's two o'clock now. Drop everything else you're working on and do some background research on the bidding process. Talk to people who have submitted bids in the past. See if they ever suspected anything. Then check the background of Braynard Construction with the Better Business Bureau. Has the company ever been accused of anything illegal? Have any complaints ever been made? Check everything. Once you have the telephone records, then we begin interviewing the key players. I'd like to run with this story for Wednesday's front page."

"I'll hurry," I said.

I spent the remainder of that day learning about bidding scams. I discovered that bid-rigging was not an unusual occurrence in the construction business, and that the federal government was not lenient when it came to racketeering. Jim Hastings called back and said the telephone records would be available the following afternoon.

"Listen, Jim," I said. "When you were talking to Mary about this incident, did you believe her?"

"Does it matter?" he asked.

"I just wondered."

Jim paused for a moment. "Let's wait for the records."

On Tuesday afternoon I phoned the sheriff's office and asked for Deputy Hastings.

"Well?" I asked.

"I hope Mary Leighton is not too good a friend of yours," he replied. "The record shows that a call was definitely made from her phone to Braynard Construction at 4:02 p.m. on the day in question. It's pretty conclusive."

"Thanks, Jim," I said and reached for my car keys.

The Leighton home was a split-level on the east side of town. The front yard was moderately sized and sloped down to a driveway and a two-car garage. I had noticed as I drove up that the back yard was fenced. Was this the residence of a corrupt city worker? I asked myself. It seemed to fit the Leightons' economic status; there was nothing pretentious about the place. A boy's bicycle lay carelessly on its side near the front steps.

I walked up to the front door and knocked. Jeff Leighton answered and gazed at me suspiciously.

"Hello, Jeff," I said.

"Donny," he replied and gazed nervously down the street.

I wondered what he was looking for.

"I think you can guess why I'm here," I said sympathetically. "Is Mary home?"

Jeff pressed his hand to the door. "Look, Donny," he said. "I don't think this is the time . . ."

I held on to the doorknob. "It's past the time, Jeff," I said. "Maybe I can help."

The look of defiance quickly burned out of his eyes, and he let the door swing open. I stepped into the living room and saw Mary's two little girls playing with dolls on the floor. Her son was drawing at a table in the dining room.

Mary came into the room and sat on the couch. She was a small young woman with curly chestnut hair and dark, almost black eyes. I had always thought of her as Italian, but she could have been Spanish or Greek. Now she looked tired and there were dark smudges under her eyes. From a distance she looked like a teenager, but when I got up close, I saw the strain of years.

"I never made that call, Donny," Mary pleaded, her voice trembling. "Never."

"The sheriff has the phone records," I offered quietly. "A call was made from your phone to Braynard Construction at 4:02 p.m. on Friday. Witnesses have placed you at your desk at that time. Stan Drussell heard you . . ."

Mary began to cry.

I picked up a box of Kleenex from the coffee table and handed it to her.

"Will you get my Bible, Jeff?" she asked her husband.

Jeff found the Bible and brought it to her. Mary placed her hand on the cover and gazed at me. "I promise before God and all that is righteous, Donny, that I didn't make that call," she said.

"Okay," I muttered. She and her husband had attended the First Assembly Church of Eden Springs for three years, and I had seen them in times of worship and prayer. It was in this way that I trusted her—or at least did not distrust her motives.

"Then we have to find out what happened," I suggested. "Let's walk through the whole afternoon step by step."

As the two little girls played on the floor, Mary discussed her movements in and out of the office that Friday afternoon. She had returned from lunch at half past twelve. At three she had taken a break, sitting outside on a bench with another secretary to enjoy the sunshine. She was back upstairs fifteen minutes later. At four o'clock Stan Drussell had come out of his office, glanced at the wall clock, and exclaimed in a huff, "It's already four o'clock and I haven't gotten a thing done. There are so many meetings."

"Did anyone else hear him say this?" I interrupted.

"The other secretary was there," Mary said. "Her desk is just across the office."

"So she told the sheriff you were at your desk at four o'clock?"

"That's right."

"Did she hear you make the call?"

"No. She only said that I was at my desk. She was busy with her own work and wasn't paying any attention to what I was doing."

I glanced at the two little girls. They both had their mother's dark curly hair and dark eyes.

"It doesn't sound very good, does it?" her husband asked nervously, sitting beside Mary.

I shook my head.

"I just don't understand," Mary cried. "Why would Stan Drussell say I made that call when I didn't? Why would the records show that a call had been made from my desk when it wasn't?"

"I don't know," I said.

"Have you spoken with Mr. Carper from Braynard Construction? He says he didn't talk to me. He doesn't know any more about it than I do."

"He's next on my list," I offered.

"Talk to him," Jeff urged. "He'll tell you the same thing."

"I'll try," I promised. "If . . ."

"If what?" Mary asked.

"If I can get through his lawyer. He isn't making any statements at the moment."

Six

~

A yellow sticky was on my computer when I returned to the Banner. A name and number were written across the small yellow square. The handwriting was feminine, so it must have been taken by Thomas's secretary.

"And this is . . . ?" I asked, walking into the editor's office.

"A guy who works for Kaplan Construction," Thomas said. "He wants to talk to you about the bids."

"Why?" I asked. "Doesn't he know his company will probably get the contract now that Braynard is being investigated?"

"Who knows?" Thomas said. "Anyway, see what he has to say."

As I punched in the numbers on my telephone, I thought of Sylvie. I had been thinking about my cousin all morning, thinking that there was something I wanted to tell her, some wisdom I had to impart, but whatever shred of advice I had to share had not yet reached a cognizant level. For the moment it rested just below my consciousness in the form of uneasiness—or was it worry? Perhaps if I had had the time to think about it, I could have worked it out rationally. But emotions were never that practical—at least not mine.

"Hello," a voice said on the other end of the telephone. It was a gruff voice with an edge of contempt, which surprised me, because I could have been anyone calling. Perhaps he was expecting someone else.

"This is Don Foster with the Eden Springs Banner," I explained. "May I speak with Clifton Howard?"

"This is Cliff," the voice said, softening from contempt into simple disdain. "You a reporter?"

"Yes," I said. "I understand that you had a comment about the proposal bids."

He gave a short laugh. "If that's what you call 'em."

"I'd like to hear about that," I said. "You're an employee of Kaplan Construction?"

"Manager."

"Well, Mr. Howard, before you say anything, I would like to tape this conversation. Is that all right with you?"

There was a pause. "I'd rather not do it this way," he said. "Couldn't we meet somewhere?"

"Wherever you like," I responded.

Another pause.

"Okay," he said at last. "I'll meet you at the entrance to River Trail Park at half past three."

"I'll be there," I said and hung up.

It seemed to me as I drove out the narrow two-lane blacktop to River Trail Park that there were varying levels of truth on any given subject. There was a side of me that felt guilty for not becoming a pastor as I had planned when I was younger, but another side of me was pleased with being a reporter. After all, in a way they were both professions of reform. Tag had told me he was all right, and in some ways that was true, and in others obviously not. Also, his promise to take care of Sylvie was only partially true, for a man in love with a woman invariably does things that are desired and yet are not in her best interest. Melissa wanted to believe that Sylvie was an innocent, and perhaps that was true in her mind, but it had long since been untrue physically. So there were varying levels of truth in everything except the Scripture. Then it was not a question of varying levels of truth but varying levels of understanding. Sometimes I felt that my understanding of the scriptural truth changed from day to day so that my application of the truth varied also. It was something I kept in the back of my mind in moments like this.

A new Ford pickup truck was parked at the entrance to the River Trail area. As I pulled over, I saw a man leaning against the back of the truck. He was about fifty with curly gray hair and a mustache.

"Foster?" he inquired in the same gruff voice I had heard over the telephone.

"Yes," I replied.

He gazed around the park.

"Nice, isn't it?"

I nodded.

"We really wanted this job," he said. "It's hard to stay in business in a small town like Eden Springs."

I felt myself growing impatient. I hadn't left the office to hear another complaint about the restrictions of small-town life.

"Well, Mr. Howard," I said, "it looks like you'll get the contract. The City Council disqualified Braynard Construction."

"Right," he said. "I read about that in the paper."

We walked through the stone gated entrance and up the narrow pavement. To my right was a wide field that sloped down to a wooded area by the river. On the left was a park pavilion with picnic tables. The park wound along for another mile beside the river.

"The big money isn't here," Howard explained. "The park improvements are just trivial stuff—drainage and sewage. The big money is in the Cottonwood Road expansion."

"I can imagine," I offered.

"I worked real hard on that bid, trying to trim costs so we could get the contract. When I put it in, I was sure we had the lowest numbers. I factored the profit margin at 18 percent. Most companies figure 35 percent profit."

"But you weren't the only two," I reminded him. "There was another contractor from the capital."

"Sure," Howard said. "I know about them. But they're big-city. They pay higher wages. They couldn't afford to bid a contract for less than our company."

"So what are you saying, Mr. Howard?" I asked.

Clifton Howard stopped walking and gazed across the fields to the trees and the river.

"I've heard you're a friend of Mary Leighton's," he said slowly. "And being a reporter, you could cause trouble if you kept the investigation going—maybe slow down the process."

"Listen, Mr. Howard," I said sternly. "I report the news as factually and fairly as possible. Whatever happens after that—well, it happens."

"I know," Howard said. "But now that we have a chance to get this contract, I hope you won't do anything to screw it up. I'm counting on your professional integrity."

"There's no question about my integrity, Mr. Howard," I snapped.

"Sure," he said and spat.

I saw Sylvie again when I stopped by my uncle's house to drop off a set of jumper cables. She was folding her laundry at the kitchen table.

"I thought you had your own apartment," I said.

"I moved in with Melissa to save money . . . but our washer is broken."

"How's Tag?"

She casually folded a gray T-shirt and placed it neatly on her pile of clothes. The shirt had AIR FORCE in black letters across the front. Had it been a gift, I wondered, or was she now doing Tag's laundry?

"Don't you know, Donny?" she asked.

I didn't like the implication behind that question, but I didn't say anything. I deserved as much for getting involved in her business.

"I haven't seen him since he went back to work," I said defensively.

Sylvie must have noticed the expression on my face.

"I'm not trying to be mean," she said. "I know the two of you are good friends."

"I never see much of Tag when he's involved with someone," I admitted. I didn't say this to hurt her—at least I didn't think so—but it was true. When Tag was in a relationship, the rest of the world ceased to exist for him.

"Oh," Sylvie replied in a hurt voice. "Then I imagine you've seen him this way before."

"From time to time."

She folded a pair of blue jeans thoughtfully and placed them on the pile. I couldn't help glancing at the label and noticing that they were a woman's brand. The T-shirt must have been a gift.

"And I suppose these relationships follow a typical pattern?"

"They used to," I said, not feeling that I was betraying the past. "But Tag has changed a lot since he joined the Air Force. I never know how he is going to act anymore."

Sylvie looked at me closely. In return, I tried to look as encouraging as possible.

"Really," I stressed.

"Well, then," she sighed and folded two white socks together. "Why don't we all go out for a pizza or something?"

"Anne is off tomorrow night," I suggested.

Sylvie thought for a moment. "Tag is going bowling right after work tomorrow evening," she said. "But we could meet you at the bowling alley at seven o'clock. We could go out for something then."

"Okay," I said. "I'll ask Anne."

"That would be fine," she said. "Tag will be calling in a few minutes. I'll talk to him about it."

As I drove away from her house in the late afternoon —a time of day I generally disliked in summer, that transitional period between four and six when the heat of day seems to press down before it is tempered into a promise of evening coolness—I felt that Sylvie had other reasons for her invitation. Did she want to see how Tag acted in the company of old friends? I wondered. Would that give her a better perspective on his character? Or did she want me to see them together? Would I, in her eyes, drop any reservations I might have once I saw them holding hands, or leaning shoulder to shoulder at the table? I knew what Anne would say: that I was being too analytical, that I had to have an answer for every

question and to know the motive behind every action.
And that was true; most of the time I did think that way.
But how else can you move through life with any feeling
of understanding, unless you try to comprehend the
actions of the people around you? To me, it seemed only
natural.

Seven

~

A t the intersection of Twenty-first Street, I turned right on an impulse and headed east past the medical clinic. Turning onto Highland Avenue, I immediately saw the old house. This was the residence where my mother had grown up, where Grandfather and Grandmother Graham had lived for nearly thirty years. The house was so much a part of me that it did not seem possible it could be owned by strangers now. The once-clean white wood frame was a dingy yellow. The steps I had helped my grandfather to build, my grandfather looking on as I stirred the cement, were now cracked and worn. The front porch where my parents had held their wedding reception was rotted and sagging. I pulled my Trooper over to the curb and stopped. I hadn't been past here in about a year. Just there on the back porch was where my grandfather had given me my first haircut. My mother had cried, realizing that an irretrievable moment had passed in her son's life, that I was no longer a baby. And my grandfather had laughed, standing there in his sleeveless T-shirt with the clippers and comb in his hands.

Through the back door Great-Grandmother Graham, old and mentally unstable by then, used to chase my grandmother out of the house with a broom, my grand-mother yelling, "Harry, Harry," and my grandfather taking the old, senile woman aside and talking to her gently until she calmed down.

In the alley was a cinder-block garage where my grandfather had kept his fishing rods. He always said we would go fishing one day, but we never did. We had planned to go many times, and then he became ill and lost weight. Standing at his bedside, I had seen his frail, ashen face and weak smile and realized that our chance to go fishing had passed. I had not really understood death then. I did not know that the worst part of death was the longing—the longing to hear the voice, the smile, the touch of gentle hands, to hear the stories about my mother when she was young, and how it was to grow up when all this was nothing more than cornfields and dirt roads.

My mother had not talked much about her youth, but I do know that her family had fallen on lean times. My grandfather had worked for the railroad as a brakeman when he could, but he did not secure a steady position until he became a conductor during World War II. So he had scrounged at odd jobs, selling shoe polish, matches, anything to bring in a few dollars. It didn't take a lot of money to survive in those days, but even a dollar was hard to come by. It put a physical strain on him, trying to support a wife and five children. He had been out of work for a month when he came home one day all excited and told my grandmother that he had found a job. When she asked him where, he had replied, "At the glass factory."

My grandmother had been trying to make ends meet by stretching their meager savings this way and that, and she couldn't have been happier that her husband had found work. Yet the mention of the glass factory caused her to cringe inwardly. A lump formed in her slender throat. "The glass factory, Harry?" she had asked.

The glass factory in Cedarville was the Devil's own inferno on earth. If there had been any extra weight on my grandfather's lean frame, it would not have lasted long. The work was hard and grimy, and the temperatures exceeded what a man could normally bear for eight or ten hours a day.

But they had managed somehow.

My grandmother told me a story about those days. She had asked my grandfather for money, just a few coins to buy a piece of meat or potatoes for dinner that evening. My grandfather, a gentle man with a sensitive, religious heart, had shown pain in his eyes as he reached into the pocket of his trousers.

"I only got a dime, Bets," he said. "That's all the money I got in the world—just this one dime." He had handed the small coin over to my grandmother.

My grandmother loved her husband and knew how hard he was trying to provide for his family. "Fine, Harry," she had said without hesitation. She opened her coin purse as if he had given her a silver dollar and pulled off her apron.

"Mind the kids," she said.

It was only a short walk down Highland Avenue to the butcher shop on Shelby Street. There was another, larger shop on Oak Street, where my grandmother could have gone for a better selection of meats, but having only the dime and knowing the butcher on Shelby Street by name, she chose to go there.

She told me time and again about the window of the butcher shop that morning and how there were displayed a variety of roasts, chickens, liver, and sausages, and how she had stood there for a long time and felt like crying—thinking of her five children at home. But she only had the dime, and there wasn't any changing that, so she set her mind and opened the shop door. She walked inside with an air of careless abandon (she was always a spunky one) and browsed over the counter as if she just couldn't decide exactly what she wanted.

The butcher, Mr. Weaver, was waiting on another customer. When he looked up from his chopping block, he called, "Hello, Mrs. Graham. How are you today?"

"Very well, Mr. Weaver," my grandmother said, placing her hand against the cool glass of the counter.

After the other customer had paid and gone out of the shop, the butcher came over to where my grandmother was waiting.

"What can I get for you today, Mrs. Graham?" he asked.

My grandmother shook her head. In those days she had very fine, auburn hair, which she wore in tight curls.

"Well," she said. "My neighbor gave me a recipe for a new soup, and I'd love to try it. Have you got a good soup bone?"

"Of course," the butcher nodded. He opened a box behind the counter and held up a large bone. The bone was fresh and white and covered with bits of meat.

"Will this do, Mrs. Graham?"

"Yes," my grandmother said, smiling. "That would be fine, Mr. Weaver."

The butcher wrapped the bone in a piece of slick brown paper.

"Will that be all for today?" he asked.

"I believe so," my grandmother had said.

The butcher checked the weight of the bone on his scale. "That will be fifteen cents, Mrs. Graham," he said, gazing at the arrow on the scale.

My grandmother opened her bag and took out her coin purse. Within the coin purse was a sewing thimble, a button off one of her boy's shirts, and the dime. She took out the dime and held it in her hand. The tiny bit of silver felt even smaller in her fingers. The butcher waited patiently. My grandmother looked up questioningly.

"That was fifteen cents," the butcher repeated, in response to her look of puzzlement.

"Yes," my grandmother smiled again. She placed the dime on the countertop. It made a small 'clink' as it settled on the glass.

The butcher began to say something. "That was . . ." but then he gazed at my grandmother, and his voice dropped. There was a look of sweet desperation on her face.

"Thank you, Mr. Weaver," my grandmother said politely.

The butcher took the coin and dropped it into his cash register.

"And you know, Donny," my grandmother told me years later. "I put that bone in the pot with the few vegetables we had managed to scrape together, and that was the best soup I ever tasted. The Lord's love is unfailing. Yes, it is."

Hearing that story as a child, I had prayed that there was something of my grandparents in me, some quality that had remained undiluted and could be called upon in times of stress. That time had come sooner than I had expected.

The room where my grandfather had been ill was the same room where, several years earlier, I had slipped out of bed late one Christmas Eve and had waited expectantly behind a stuffed chair all through the night for Santa Claus to arrive and place our presents under the tree. But Santa did not come, and it was at that moment, squatting on the hardwood floor in the cold morning light coming through the white lace curtains, that I had stopped believing in Christmas. I had gone back to bed then and slipped under the quilt beside my cousin Philipp. I didn't say anything later when we got up and the presents were under the tree. I didn't say anything because I didn't want to spoil the holiday for him.

Even at the age of eight I had felt an almost paternal responsibility for the happiness of others. I knew that was a joke, of course, that we could not be responsible for the happiness of anyone but ourselves. Yet I felt compelled to try. I hoped that someone out there was at that moment considering my happiness—and I knew someone was—at least in a spiritual sense.

Eight

~

I sat up late Tuesday night, trying to figure out how such a sweet young woman as Mary Leighton, so obviously caught in the act, could be innocent. Yet I believed her to be innocent. It was her use of the word *immoral* that settled the matter for me. She had said that she would never be involved in anything immoral. Illegality was a transient and subjective term, but immorality was a constant. So I believed her. In accepting her version of the story, though, I had to change my perspective on what had happened.

Eventually, I decided the problem was rather simple. Mary was telling the truth; therefore, Stan Drussell had to be lying. Taking out a notepad, I jotted down Mary's name. Then I jotted down the name of Drussell. I drew a line from Mary's name to Drussell's and then to . . . to what? What was the next connection? If Drussell was lying, then what was his motive? Who had made the call? And how could it have been made from Mary's telephone without her knowledge?

It was only a short walk the next morning from the Banner to the new addition behind the courthouse which held the City Works Department. On my way, I worked through the questions I wanted to ask Drussell. Entering the building, I saw that the office was located on the second floor. I took the stairs and found it at the end of the hallway. A secretary glanced up at me as I entered and said, "Yes?" with perhaps the most apathetic tone I had ever heard. I was immediately put off. The office was cluttered with stacks of papers and files. I wondered how Mary Leighton could have managed to work in such an unpleasant environment. I gave the secretary my name and asked if I could speak to Drussell. While she was getting him, I glanced curiously around the office. There were three desks in a row and then an open door to which Drussell's name was attached. Mary Leighton's desk must have been the last one, I told myself.

After a moment, a slender man with thinning brown hair stepped out of the office and approached me. He had the ashen complexion of a heavy smoker, and I noticed a nicotine stain on his right index finger. He squinted at me defensively and smiled, showing bad teeth. I wondered if the City Works Department had a dental plan.

"Mr. Foster," he said. "You're a reporter with the Banner?"

"Yes," I replied, showing my press card. "I wondered if I could ask you a few questions?"

"In regards to what?" he asked.

I glanced at the secretary. "Could we step into your office?"

"Yes, of course."

I followed him into the office and seated myself on a metal chair across from his desk. He sat with his arms folded and gazed at me questioningly.

"We're doing a story on the bidding scam, and I wondered if you would like to make a comment," I said.

Drussell held a hand up to his mouth and shook his head. I could only imagine what he was thinking.

"There's nothing much to it, Mr. Foster," he replied. "I heard Mary talking to someone on the phone about the bids—giving them the figures, you know. That's illegal, so I reported her. We have a good name at the City Works office."

"Really?" I asked.

The hand moved over his mouth again. "Really."

"Can you remember exactly what she said?"

Drussell stood up and walked to the door. "You'll have to excuse me, Mr. Foster, but I have an appointment."

"Surely you want to set the record straight," I said. "The scandal occurred under your supervision."

"I'm very sorry," he said more sternly.

I could feel his eyes, and those of his secretary, burning holes in my back as I crossed the office. When I was in the corridor again, I took a deep breath and relaxed. There was definitely something unpleasant about Stan Drussell. It emanated from him like the cigarette smoke that clung to his clothing. I glanced at my watch. It was half past three. I still had time for another interview. Taking the stairs again, I headed up to the third floor and the mayor's office.

It seemed as if time passed in slow motion until the story was complete—or as complete as it could be in the rush of a few hours—for human emotions and motives have no place in a news story. As expected, the mayor and the chairman of the City Council were outraged. The story ran on page one under the headline:

Allegations of Misconduct in Cottonwood Bids

I realized the story would continue now for weeks, perhaps even months, until some kind of resolution was reached. Each time it appeared in the Banner it would receive fewer lines of text and a higher page number until finally it would be buried across from the classified section. In the meantime, I decided to learn more about the three construction companies that had submitted bids. I also would check the backgrounds of Drussell, Leighton, and Phil Carper, manager of Braynard Construction. I knew it would take time, but I was not in any hurry to change my opinion of Eden Springs. Perhaps I was as guilty as Melissa of wanting to pretend that we still existed in the garden. In some ways we did, after all, for wasn't it a question of desire? Hadn't the decision to live in the garden been a choice, and didn't we still have that choice—made over and over again on a daily basis through strength of faith? I thought so, but it was a difficult balance to maintain, and I felt myself slipping every day in one direction or another.

We met Tag and Sylvie that evening at Pizza Hut. They had just come from the bowling alley, and Tag was wearing his bowling team shirt. It made me think of all the uniforms we wear in life—some physical and some spiritual. Sylvie looked especially vibrant and was trying her best to make everyone have a good time. I wondered why it was so important to her that Anne and I have a good time—but perhaps she wasn't doing it for us. Perhaps she wanted to give this little piece of happiness to Tag, adding a piece here and there until it eventually formed a whole experience of happiness and became a part of his life.

I told them about Mary Leighton and how it was essentially over as a news story, but that it continued to bother me. So many stories passed through the newspaper and then ended, with the implication that it was also over for the persons involved. This was often not the case. Even if Mary was only put on probation, she had already lost her job, and now she would have a federal charge in her file.

"It seems simple enough to me," Sylvie offered as the waitress brought our pizza. "Someone else made the call on an extension phone. That would work, wouldn't it? If they hooked up a line to Mary's?"

"An extension phone?" I said. "I hadn't thought about that."

"Who would notice in an office?" Anne commented. "I have no idea where our phone lines at the hospital are attached."

"I suppose it's possible," I said. "What do you think, Tag?"

Tag took a bite of his pizza and thought for a moment. "If the phone was in Drussell's office, he would have to hide it somehow."

"Yes," Sylvie said, smiling. "He couldn't just suddenly have another phone on his desk."

"Wouldn't it ring every time Mary got a call?" Anne suggested.

I thought about that for a moment.

"He would only use it the one time," I said. "Then he would unplug it and put it away."

Sylvie smiled delightedly. "You didn't know what you were missing in the Air Force, Tag. All this mystery."

Tag shook his head.

"It's just one exciting story after another," I quipped.

Anne sighed. "Well, now that we've solved the problem, how about going for a walk when we're finished?"

"Down Fifth Street to the square?" Sylvie offered.

"Okay," I said.

We walked in couples, with Tag and Sylvie in the lead. It was a clear summer night, and I caught a hint of something in the breeze, a subtle whiff of happiness and the scent of overwhelming desire and excitement for life to come. I had not sensed that emotion or noticed that promise in the air for several years. It blew across the quiet streets and railroad tracks of Eden Springs now as we moved hand in hand, and I was happy that we had decided to walk.

"Can you feel that?" I asked Anne.

"Yes," she said and put her arm through mine.

Nine

~

Anne Perrault.

The funny thing was that a group of us had gone out for dinner because Tony Hamilton was in town. That was a year ago now. I didn't know Tony all that well—his family owned the local Ford dealership, and we had traveled in different circles. But he was a friend of an editor on the Banner, so I had tagged along. A few young women had been invited too, and one of them was Anne. My first impression, as I gazed at her from across the starched white tablecloth and the expanse of silverware and plates, was of a young woman with a remarkable smile—beautiful teeth enhanced by the flickering candlelight—and striking brown eyes. She wore her hair short then. I wanted to talk to her, but everyone was focused on Tony. He had recently inherited a mansion in Chicago from an uncle. It was said to have a ballroom on the second floor. I wanted to ask him how it felt to live in such a palace, but was warned not to mention it. "Tony gets upset if you ask questions about his house," someone confided in me. "He's sick to death of hearing about it."

"So soon?" I asked. "Wasn't that just a year ago?"

The confidant nodded earnestly. "You'll never hear from him again if you bring up the mansion."

"I'll try to remember."

The evening had passed slowly.

"So we were in Antibes, and a friend was explaining that a sailboat is nothing more than a hole you throw money into, and I was . . ." Tony was expounding.

We had already heard about Monaco and Cannes, so I tuned him out and gazed at Anne. She smiled at me and raised her dark eyebrows. So, I thought happily, she wasn't impressed either.

"Excuse me, Tony," I said, interrupting. "I've heard there's a ballroom on the second floor of your new mansion. Is that true?"

Our host glared at me.

"I suppose so," Tony replied with disdain, and I could see the others shaking their heads at me sympathetically. Poor small town boy just didn't know how to behave around the rich.

It was time to make the final move. Glancing at my watch, I said, "Gosh, it's getting late. If you'll excuse me, I have to be at work early tomorrow morning."

Tony smiled superficially and dismissed me with a wave. I glanced at Anne.

"I'm Donny Foster," I said, offering her my hand.

Anne laughed. "I know," she said. "I'm a friend of Melissa's."

"My cousin? Really?" I asked, studying her face more closely. I was certain that I had never seen her before.

Anne smiled again. "I've been gone for a while."

"Got tired of small town life, eh?" I said cynically.

"Not at all," she said. "I was in nurse's training."

"A nurse?"

"Yes."

"And now you're back? You live in Eden Springs?"

"I work at the hospital."

Tony shot me an angry glance. I was interrupting his story—something about ordering *paella* at a restaurant in Nice.

"Well," I said. "Any friend of Melissa's . . ."

Anne looked at her watch. "I should be going, too."

"Do you need a ride?"

"If it's not too much trouble."

"No trouble at all," I said sincerely. "I'd be happy to."

I escorted her out to the Trooper, and she gave me directions for my first trip to Genesee Street. On the way, I found out very quickly about her faith. With some people the very air they breathe reminds them of God— causes them to ponder the ways of creation—and so it was with Anne. She had a simple but profound faith, the depths of which I couldn't even imagine. I felt like an incorrigible sinner seated next to her as she talked. I *was* an incorrigible sinner, after all, but sometimes I imagined myself to be just a bit above the average man on the street. With Anne Perrault, however, my shortcomings were all too evident. I began to squirm with guilt.

"It's just here," she said and pointed to a stone house with a wide porch. A small gate led up to the front steps. I knew at once that I would love this place. Even at night, there was a sense of warmth and comfort, as if the very stones had been set with affection. Across the street was a potato field that stretched away into the darkness. It seemed as if Anne's house were the last point of light before a vast and ominous void. Perhaps it was—in my life, anyway.

"Well, I'm glad you're a friend of Melissa's," I said again, foolishly. Why was I suddenly having so much trouble? I was usually quite confident around women. I told myself that I didn't know why, but I knew. You don't often come in contact with an angel.

The summer moved on quickly, and soon it was the Fourth of July, a holiday that always crept up on me and for which I was always unprepared. Some of my friends had purchased fireworks weeks in advance, but I always put it off—and I began to wonder if that wasn't some form of denial on my part. For me, the Fourth of July was the apogee of that hot season which began in late May and arched back into August. There was only one place to be on that summer evening, and that was down at the riverbank to watch the fireworks. Anne and I had taken a picnic dinner and spread out a blanket behind the Trooper. As the fading light cast shadows on the water, we lay back on the blanket and gazed up at the darkening sky.

Anne gazed up at Venus. "First star I see tonight," she whispered.

"What are you thinking about?" I asked, with my hands folded behind my head.

I felt her soft hair brush against my cheek in the darkness. "I can't tell you," she said. "It won't come true."

Across the river there was a crackling thud, and the first fireworks shot into the sky.

"They're beginning."

I gazed up at the sparkling blue and red burst with a feeling of overwhelming peacefulness. The blanket was comfortable beneath me, Anne was nestled at my side, and the night air held the hint of a memory which came back to me from long ago. Lying there, I suddenly remembered when I was eight years old and Grandpa Foster had brought me out here in his old black Plymouth. I could still recall the scratchy brown upholstery of the seats and the hot-radiator smell of the interior; that very old car smell which I now, for some reason, associated with loneliness and depression. Any time I got into a car that smelled of old heat and radiator fumes, that sense of depression instantly enveloped me. Why? I wondered. Had I, in some childish way, been ashamed of my paternal grandfather? Had I sensed his weakness, his bitterness, his lack of accomplishment in life? Or were there odors in life which could not be taken in any other context than with a feeling of sadness? Those days seemed so long ago, and yet nothing had changed: The river still lay flat and dark below us, our blanket was spread out on the same rocky bank, and the stars that glowed down upon us were constant. I began to feel a sense of my life being one enveloping moment that had no beginning or end, but was just now—as if everything transpired at the same time—and I thought if I just imagined hard enough Mother would be here, and Dad too, and even Grandpa, and I wouldn't have to experience this loneliness and sense that there was always something more out there, something that I was missing, that I was somehow not able to understand, something not so far away as God but which served as an emotional intermediary.

A firework exploded into a glistening ball of gold and green. I put my arm around Anne.

"I'm glad you're here," I said.

She snuggled closer to me. "Me too."

Another firework burst overhead, and then another and another for thirty minutes until the bombastic, visually and colorfully overpowering finale.

I was just sitting up on the blanket and listening to the people near us packing to leave when someone called my name.

"Donny?"

There were cars parked all along the bank, but I hadn't seen anyone I knew.

"Donny?" the voice came again, this time from behind the Trooper.

I stood up. "Over here."

A slender form appeared in the darkness.

"Sylvie," I said. "I didn't know you were coming out here tonight."

A pair of headlights from a passing car swept across her for a moment, and I could see concern on her face.

"I saw your Trooper," she said. "Hello, Anne."

"Is something wrong?" Anne asked, giving Sylvie a hug.

"Well," she said, and hesitated. "I'm not sure."

"Tag?" I asked.

"I don't think he had that much to drink," she explained. "At least not while I've been with him. But..."

"Where's your car?" I asked.

"We're parked over there," she said and pointed into the darkness.

I took a flashlight out of my glove compartment, and we followed Sylvie back to her car. When we arrived, I saw Tag slumped in the seat behind the steering wheel. He gave a start when I tapped his shoulder and mumbled something, but then slumped again and closed his eyes.

"What's he been drinking?" I asked.

"A few beers," Sylvie noted. "That's all. I'm trying to get him to stop, you know. He's been doing so much better."

I looked around. Most of the cars had left now, except for a few that would be lingering until the small hours of the night. A cool wind was beginning to blow in from the river.

"This is no good," I said. "We've got to get him home."

"I tried to move him," Sylvie said. "But he's too heavy."

I leaned into the car and put my arm around Tag's shoulders. He was heavy. "Come on, buddy," I urged.

Tag opened his eyes slowly. "Hey, Donny," he muttered and smiled wearily. "Didn't get me . . . didn't get me, Donny."

"Who didn't get you?" I asked, pulling him toward me and out of the car.

"No more Bear," he muttered and closed his eyes again. "Just like that. Pieces . . . pieces."

I looked at Sylvie. "Do you know what he's talking about?"

She shook her head.

"If you can hold him, I'll go and get the Trooper," Anne offered.

I handed her the flashlight and keys and watched as she moved down the bank. Then I pushed the car door shut with my hip, and leaned Tag against the side.

Sylvie patted his cheek tenderly. "You think he's all right?" she asked.

"He's just had a bit too much," I said. "I'm sure he'll be fine in the morning."

"I hope so," she replied. "He has to work in the morning."

"In this condition?"

"He tried to get the day off, but the chief told him it was impossible."

"Why?"

"It's the Air Force," she stated, as if that would answer all my questions.

And of course, it did.

Ten

~

hen Anne returned with the Trooper, we decided it would be best if I drove Tag home while Sylvie and Anne followed in her car. My anger and disappointment in Tag were beginning to change into concern. This was certainly not the same friend who had gone off to serve in the Gulf War. What had happened to him? I felt that Mrs. Taggart knew the answers to these questions, and I was determined to ask her. But when I pulled up in front of the Taggart house, the lights were out. I glanced at my watch. It was after eleven. Sylvie and Anne parked behind me and came up to my window.

"What do you want to do?" I asked Sylvie. "It looks like Mrs. Taggart has already gone to bed."

"There's a house key under the geranium," she said with an air of familiarity that surprised me. "Can you help?"

"Sure," I said and climbed out. I hoisted Tag up in a kind of half-carry, half-drag position and we began to move up the sidewalk. Just then, the porch lights flicked on. So Mrs. Taggart was awake, I thought, and I wondered if she always kept this nightly vigil when Tag was out, tip-toeing silently to bed when she saw that her son had returned safely.

The front door opened.

"He's okay," I called quickly, not wanting to alarm her. "Just a little too much celebrating."

"Oh, my," she sighed. "This is so kind of you, Donny. You're such a good friend."

I was beginning to have my doubts about how good a friend I was, but I didn't say anything. The stairs leading up to Tag's bedroom on the second floor were too narrow, so we put him on the bed in the guest room. Sylvie pulled a sheet over him.

"That's okay, honey," Mrs. Taggart said to her. "I can take care of him."

I saw that Sylvie wanted to stay, but there was really no point in remaining. Tag would sleep now until morning. She was quiet as we walked back to the cars. I could only imagine what she was thinking. Was she weighing the odds of a future with someone in Tag's condition? Was that female practicality involved? Or was she planning a course in redemption, working out the strategies of a permanent cure for this obviously messed-up young man? It seemed totally out of place for me to ask.

"I'm worried about Tag," Anne said as we drove to her house. "How long has he been in this condition?"

"I don't know," I replied. "It seems to come and go."

"The drinking?"

"No, the . . ." I hesitated. How could I depict Tag's psychological state since his return. Shell shock? Panic? Post war trauma? I wasn't a psychiatrist. All I could say was that he didn't seem to be the same confident young man who had left Eden Springs sixteen months before.

"Yes, the drinking," I answered after a moment. "But there's more to it than that. He seems to suffer from these bouts of anxiety. Something like that. He won't talk about it, though. I've tried. He always says he'll tell me some other time."

"And Sylvie knows?"

"Of course."

Anne gazed at the passing streets. "She must love him a lot," she sighed.

I began to wonder about the nature of female love and what Anne was really thinking.

After dropping Anne off at her house, I returned to my apartment. It was a small place with a bedroom, living room, kitchen with breakfast nook, and bathroom. I didn't require much, except that I needed to feel that I lived near people, that there was life around me. The view of the town square from my bay window gave me the impression of being in a much larger community. In the mornings the sound of passing traffic and pedestrians on the sidewalks had an almost cosmopolitan air. I would crawl from my sheets and think. This is my Paris, my New York, the essence of who I am and what I am about. Everything I do comes from these wood-framed houses and bricked streets. Even the goals I have set for myself in life are given perimeters by the city limits of this town. And is that so bad? Should I be ashamed in some vague way for remaining in Eden Springs while others—Tag, for example—have gone off to other parts of the world and had experiences which I cannot share? Is there a reason why I am still here? Is there? Do I pray about something for which there is no real need of an answer? Is that even justified?

I thought about this as I went to bed, a pillow pressed against my lower back as a precaution against loneliness, and lay in the darkness without sleeping. The lights from a passing car moved slowly across the room and I thought, you have a fine life for yourself here, old boy. Just fine. And how much longer can you continue? How much longer can you keep up the pretense of moving forward without knowing where you are headed? But did any of us know? Yes, yes, the golden crown. But what about the loss of innocence in the people I knew and loved. What about them?

I was awakened, without knowing I had been sleeping, by the sound of a truck horn outside my window, and I opened my eyes to see gray daylight filtering through the curtains. Walking into the kitchen, I stood at the window and watched a clerk from the grocery store unloading crates of vegetables from a delivery truck. So we begin a new day, I told myself and glanced at the sky. There were no clouds; the heavy heat of summer had finally settled over the rolling hills and fields, and I could feel its pervasiveness in the air. The afternoons now would move slowly and be oppressively hot. In the kitchen I heated up a pot of coffee, but it tasted bitter and I wished I had made tea. I wasn't really in the mood for coffee this morning. And then came the usual question. It was a question I asked myself daily, and although I usually felt as if I did not receive a specific answer, it made me feel better to ask: How could I serve God?

Walking along the sidewalk to the newspaper office, I saw that the sprinklers were on in the square. I stopped for a moment and listened to the snit-snit-snit of the sprinklers as they moved from side to side, throwing out the water. Later in the day there would be children playing in the sprinklers—maybe not here in the town square, but in many of the neighborhoods—and I thought of Mary Leighton and the bicycle that lay in her front yard.

"Anything new on the Cottonwood story?" the editor asked me as I sat at my desk.

I shook my head. "Not really. I told Jim Hastings about the extension phone theory and he had it checked out, but they didn't find anything."

Ed Thomas shook his head slowly. "Sorry to hear that. I know you believe Mary."

"Yes."

"Well, something may turn up."

I tapped my pencil against my desk. "I just can't understand why anyone would do it."

Thomas gave a gruff laugh. "Are you kidding? You know how much money was involved in this bid. Even if Braynard only gave her a kick-back of one percent, that would be eighteen thousand dollars. Did you check to see if her husband had any gambling debts, overdrafts, big medical expenses, etcetera?"

"Yes," I said. "It didn't turn up anything."

"Well, then," Ed shrugged. "Maybe she just did it for the extra money."

"Yeah," I said hesitantly.

"But you don't think so . . ."

I folded my hands behind my neck and stretched. "No."

Ed waved his hand at me with an air of frustration and turned toward his office. "You trust people too much, Donny," he said. "That's your problem."

I had to laugh. Trust had nothing to do with it. But there were advantages in lack of trust; not trusting in some situations provided an unbiased perspective. At least that's what I told myself.

Eleven

~

This time I wrote:

One

When the Jeep rolled to a stop, the missionary climbed out and gazed over the bushland. From the knoll where he stood, he could see a great baobab tree rising on the plain. The plain was yellow with goldenrod and elephant grass, red with patches of exposed earth, and spotted green with stunted thorn trees. A dark shadow of the great tree was cast by the afternoon sun.

In the Jeep behind the missionary sat the foreman of the cotton company. He had been asked by his office to show the missionary around the Tehini settlement. The two men had started out north of the river and were now south of the settlement, off the road to Latourna. The afternoon sun burned on the foreman's arm where it protruded from under the Jeep canopy.

"Do you see that baobab, Mr. Potter?" the missionary asked, pointing to the tree. "That is where we will build the mission."

"The villagers should like that, Mr. Thompson," the foreman replied. He slapped at a tse-tse fly biting through his khaki shirt— the third in a matter of minutes. "Little beggars have teeth like jackals," he muttered, pinching the dusty fly between his fingers.

The missionary's shirt was sweat-stained, a damp crease running from his shoulders to his waist. Under the wide brimmed hat, *his blond hair was clipped short. His eyes were too sensitive for the harsh light, and he squinted as he looked to the horizon.*

"We are fortunate to receive such bounty," he commented.

The foreman shrugged. "You haven't lived in the bush long enough, Mr. Thompson. Africa has a bite."

"I'm sure it does, Mr. Potter," the missionary said, studying the baobab. "But the Lord will provide."

The Lord will provide. I had hoped that a complete change of location would be good for my writing. Perhaps that had been the problem with the previous chapters. But the farther I got into the story of the missionary and his attempt to build a church, the more I was getting away from the truth of what I personally knew. And the truth of what I knew was Eden Springs and its inhabitants. Everything else was only a product of my imagination. Somehow I needed to find a story that would allow me to express my affection for this river town and its surrounding countryside, and the lessons I had learned while growing up here. It had been a good life. How could I get that down on paper?

The summer days passed, each growing steadily warmer so that the hours seemed to melt together, and I no longer slept with my windows opened, lulled to sleep by the rustle of wind in the trees or the chirp of cicadas, but listened instead to the steady hum of the air conditioner. In the evenings we watched Anne's nephew play Little League baseball at the diamond behind the school, or went to an occasional film at the multiplex theater. In the afternoons I went to Hazel's, and I could eventually recite the various summer specials as if I had memorized a poem. On Monday the special was spaghetti; Tuesday, Salisbury steak; Wednesday, pork chops; Thursday, fried chicken; Friday, meatloaf. I suspected that the leftover meatloaf from Friday was put into the spaghetti sauce on Monday, but I had no proof. Nor did I have any alternative, unless I wanted to eat fast food or begin cooking lunch for myself.

One afternoon Anne and I drove out to a pond in the woods east of the Air Force base. It was one of our favorite places to picnic because we liked to watch the aircraft streaking through the air overhead. Every child in town could tell the difference between an F15 and an F16, or an A10 and an F4. The model shapes and sounds had become so much a part of our everyday existence that we could tell when an A10 was making its approach without ever looking up.

I had taken my guitar (my feeble attempt at being romantic) and was strumming a few chords as Anne opened the cooler and set out the sandwiches.

"I wrote this song for you," I said and began to play an old popular tune.

"You didn't write that," Anne said, laughing.

"Didn't I," I said. "It sounds just like you."

"What does it mean, anyway?" she asked and sang: "Falling oh so slowly, like an angel."

"I guess angels don't fall when they step off a cloud. They just float because of their wings."

"And that reminds you of me?"

"Not that part, exactly. Just the 'I'll be there to help you' part."

"Huh uh," she said and took a bite of her sandwich.

"And the line about the heart," I added hastily.

Anne put down her sandwich. "What about your heart, Donny?"

She smiled at me brightly.

"The last time I looked, I still had one," I replied.

"You know what I mean."

A flight of F16s was taking off, and I could see the first one above the trees. A pilot friend had told me that flying an F16 was like sitting on the end of a pencil because the canopy came so far down on either side. I wondered how that felt—to be going so fast and to feel so exposed.

"Did you ever feel like you were good at something but it still wasn't what God had intended for you?" I asked.

"I don't know," she said. "It seems like God has given you a gifting as a journalist. You're not afraid to ask people difficult questions. I could never do that."

I thought about this for a moment as a second F16 ripped above the treetops and seemed to fly straight up.

"How could a person's talents and their heart desires be so different?" I asked. "It's something I've never understood."

"Are they really so different?" Anne asked, and I could see that her face looked troubled. "Do you really know what your desires are, Donny?"

One of the things I appreciated most about Anne Perrault was her ability to see through the baggage we all carry around in our lives, the walls we have put up to protect ourselves from others, or to justify the untruths we tell ourselves. I say untruths here because it is less offensive than the word lie. A lie is such a harsh word, and some untruths are meant to comfort and not to harm. However, can any untruth help us in the long run? As I mentioned before, I believed there was only one truth and that was based on understanding. But what if you were not sure what was biblical truth and what was practical, day-to-day living truth? For three years now I had thought about nothing but my unrequited desire to write a book. Was that an untruth I had been telling myself to assuage my guilt for not following the path I believed God had set before me? The answer was clear enough, though I did not want to dwell on it. If I had really wanted to go to Bible seminary, wouldn't I be there right now? Hadn't I always gone directly for what I wanted when I knew exactly what that was?

The answer was unavoidable. Yes.

Through the trees I could see a third F16 taking off. Instead of rising into the sky and streaking over our heads as the others had done, it banked sharply to the right and disappeared. A second later there was a vibrating boom, and a dark cloud of smoke rose from the woods.

"I think a jet just crashed," I blurted, jumping up.

"Where?" Anne asked.

I pointed to the ball of smoke rising above the trees. A siren suddenly went off at the base.

"Let's go!" I said.

There is a curious sense of life speeding up when an accident occurs, as if you had been sitting outside the mainstream for a time, dull and complacent, and the tragedy suddenly snapped your attention back to the realities. Though I could easily see the plume of smoke rising above the trees, it was not easy to drive to the scene. If the aircraft had crashed inside the base, I could have done nothing as a reporter. But it had landed just beyond the security fence in a cornfield. I could see where it had come down, tearing a wide path in the ground before it had flipped over and started to burn.

I found a rutted dirt road that led down to the field, and we were just coming through the trees when the crash crew vehicle came screaming down from the other direction.

"Let's not go over there," Anne urged. "I don't want to see this."

"We'll just get close enough to see what's happening," I urged. "They won't let us get near the aircraft anyway."

"You promise?" Anne asked.

I turned and saw the worry on her face.

"You're a nurse," I said. "This kind of thing shouldn't bother you."

"I haven't worked in the ER for a long time," she said defensively. "And anyway, he may be dead."

"Dead," I muttered, and I suddenly realized that I knew most of the pilots at Emerson.

"Okay," I said. "I'll just try to find out what happened. You wait here in the shade."

Anne nodded, and I left the Trooper and walked across the field toward the jet.

"Stand back!" a security policeman shouted at me as I neared the wreckage. He was wearing the standard dark blue beret and fatigues.

"I'm a reporter," I explained, holding up my ID.

"It's too dangerous!" he snapped. "Now stand back!"

The narrow glass canopy was gone, apparently lost when the F16 had flipped.

"All right," I said and stepped back a few paces. "Can you at least tell me the identity of the pilot?"

The SP gave me a fierce glare. "The pilot ejected before impact."

"Really?" I said, gazing around the treetops for signs of a chute. "I didn't see anybody coming down. Where did he land?"

The SP didn't reply, but in the distance I could hear the wail of another emergency vehicle. It was not coming in our direction, so I hurried back to the Trooper.

"Who was it?" Anne asked as I climbed into the car.

"I don't know yet," I answered. "The pilot bailed out. I think he must have come down over there . . . behind those woods."

Grinding the Trooper into a lower gear, I bumped up a dirt slope and onto a gravel track that led in the direction of the sirens.

"This is big," I said excitedly to Anne. "Do you know how much an F16 costs?"

"Donny, you're being so insensitive," she said. "Aren't you worried about the poor pilot?"

"The SP said he ejected. He's probably okay."

Anne shook her head. "I have a bad feeling."

The Air Force has a term for when a parachute doesn't have enough altitude to open properly. It is called a streamer. In this case the pilot, realizing that his engine had flamed out, had gone into a thirty-degree bank rate to try and get away from the populated area of Eden Springs. He had flown his F16 down to 100 feet when he ejected. The canopy left the jet and the seat fired, but the sink rate was too fast and his chute did not fully inflate before he hit the ground. He might as well have jumped off the city water tower.

When Anne and I came out of the woods, I could see the twisted chute hung up in the trees, the cords hanging down, and the body sprawled in the grass. There was a quiet solitude to the scene, as if God had stopped the earth and said, "Hush, I've just lost one of my own. This is a moment for respect." A warm afternoon breeze rustled the cords of the parachute and moved the grass around the body. The medics began to work on the pilot—slowly at first, almost with a solemnity, and then with a frantic activity that made me realize that he must still be alive.

I didn't want to intrude, so I stood back and watched as the medics worked. Cutting away the chin straps, they carefully removed the helmet and visor. The left side of the helmet was smashed, and I assumed that no human head could have withstood a blow like that without suffering some type of trauma. I thought of a crushed skull and splintered bone fragments and I suddenly felt terrible. Then I got a clear view of the pilot's face.

"Oh, no," I muttered, with a sinking heart. They had him on a stretcher now and were moving him to the ambulance.

"Do you know him?" Anne asked.

"Yes. It's Mark Wayland."

"The pilot you play darts with?"

I nodded.

Anne watched the ambulance pull away.

"Did you see his helmet?" I asked.

"Poor Mark," she said, her voice trembling. "I feel so sorry for his family."

"He's not dead yet," I corrected her.

Anne shot me a sympathetic glance. "No," she said. "He's not dead yet."

We followed the ambulance to Eden Springs Hospital, and I phoned in the crash information to the paper. Anne talked to a nurse who said that Mark had suffered a head injury.

"Is he expected to come out of it?" I asked, but I knew from her expression that the question was foolish.

Thinking back over that afternoon, I tried to imagine what Mark Wayland had been doing while Anne and I were driving out to the pond. It seemed strange that I was sitting there tuning my guitar as he was preparing to make his final flight. But that was the nature of flying: You never knew when the unexpected might occur. Maybe that's why so many pilots I had met were technical, by-the-book kinds of guys. One pilot said he had skipped the inspection of his F16 before a flight and the crew chief commented that he would not live very long if he continued to be so irresponsible. Check it and check it and check it again—that was the Air Force policy. Perhaps that is why the nature of the accident seemed so incredible when I later discovered the cause of the flame-out.

In a small town there are relationships, and intertwinings, and coincidences, so that you never know who might be affected by an event. One of the first calls I received that evening was from Sylvie. I was surprised to hear her voice on the line—she almost never phoned me.

"I heard about the accident," she explained. "Melissa said you were there. How is Mark?"

I was surprised again. "Not good. He suffered a head injury. He's being operated on now. I didn't know you were friends."

She was quiet for a moment. "We dated a few times. Until I started going out with Tag. Then I told Mark I couldn't go out with him anymore."

"Does Tag know that?"

"Yes. Mark kept calling me, even after I told him I was dating Tag. Once he called when Tag was over at our house."

"I bet Tag didn't like that."

"No."

"Did they ever work together?" I asked. "At the skeet club they didn't seem to know each other."

Her tone was immediately suspicious. "Why would you ask me that, Donny?"

"I was just wondering."

Sylvie was quiet again.

"Tag was assigned to Mark's plane just last month," she said finally. "Does that mean anything?"

"Of course not," I said, and I hated myself for the contemptible thought that had just entered my mind.

Twelve

~

T he plume of smoke we had seen rising from the trees that afternoon was the beginning of a six-month process that would affect the lives of at least a dozen people I knew. Directly after the crash, the Air Force blocked off the site. When I drove out to the cornfield the following afternoon, I found that the wreckage had been covered with a canvas tarp and marked off with stakes and yellow police tape and was being guarded by a security detail.

Within two or three days, a Safety Investigation Board was set up. It was the job of an SIB to determine the cause of the accident and try to prevent it from happening again. A colonel served as the board president. His staff consisted of an F16 pilot who served as the safety officer; an F16 instructor who served as the pilot member; a flight surgeon; and a life support officer. Also serving on the board as a technical expert was a representative from Lockheed Martin, the company that made the F16.

The board's investigation lasted thirty days.

I don't know what I had expected as I waited for the SIB report, but the findings were tragically simple. The investigators discovered that a rag had been left under the engine cowling of the F16. Upon take-off, the rag had become caught in the fuel injector, preventing fuel supply to the engine and causing a flame-out. This is known in the Air Force as 'foreign object damage.'

"I can't believe it," I said to Anne when we learned about the report. "A multi-million dollar aircraft and it crashed because someone left a rag in the engine."

"Imagine how the poor man must feel," she said. "I would die from guilt."

"They haven't determined who did it yet," I offered.

"How can that be? After a whole month?"

"The goal of the SIB was to determine *why* the jet crashed, not *who* was responsible. Another board will be held to determine the blame."

"That's ridiculous," Anne said. "Why would the Air Force put their own men through such stress? It surely could be handled in another way."

"There must be a reason," I suggested, but I was worried about Tag. There were only two ground crewmen on Mark Wayland's F16: the crew chief, Technical Sergeant Roy Dwyer, and the assistant crew chief, Senior Airman Richard Taggart. I assumed that one of them had inadvertently left the rag under the cowling, and I prayed every night that it was not my best friend. The guilty man would be discharged from the Air Force and face criminal charges. (A court-martial had already been scheduled for one year after the accident.) Whoever was found guilty would have to wait until next summer to face sentencing. That was an incredibly long time, and I could only imagine the pressures he would experience. I didn't want to believe Tag was responsible, yet I couldn't help thinking of his condition on the Fourth of July and Sylvie saying that he had to work the following morning. The following day was not the date of the accident—it had been weeks later—but it was obvious that Tag had sometimes gone to work when he should have stayed home. There also was the fact that Mark Wayland had dated Sylvie and had continued to call her, but I assumed that was trivial.

The Banner carried news updates on the investigation and Mark Wayland's slow recovery. Head traumas were always serious, and the prognosis was uncertain: Hopefully he would recover completely, but he might also be partially paralyzed, or slow of speech and thought. It would take months to know. In the meantime, he had been moved out of intensive care to a hospital room. Anne and I went to visit him, and I kept a tight hold on myself, whistling softly under my breath as a distraction. I hated hospitals, and just walking into one made me nervous. Every time I glanced into a hospital room, I expected to see my father lying there.

The gossip was soon flying around Eden Springs: Hadn't that Taggart boy been acting odd since his return from the Gulf? they all said, and Wasn't it rumored that Roy Dwyer had a fondness for beer? And by the way, wasn't his wife unsociable? Did you see her at the church picnic? No? Why, she wasn't even there. Those Dwyers make their appearance on Sunday and get home as fast as they can. And it's not even football season. If there was a football game on television, that would be another thing, but this is July!

And so the investigation continued.

One evening I pushed open the downstairs door to my apartment and stepped out to the sidewalk. It had rained earlier in the day, but now the setting sun cast long shadows on the sycamore trees in the square. The air felt cooler, and the sidewalks smelled damp. In another half-hour there would be fireflies in the park. Turning to my left, I headed up the sidewalk past the bank. I was thinking about Tag and the crash investigation, and of balance—of the metaphorical action of putting one step in front of the other as we tread with diligence over the traps of life, the depressions, sufferings, failures, and promises that make up our personal Via Dolorosa (the road Jesus walked on His way to the crucifixion).

Most of the shops were closed on the square, and people were moving toward the park pavilion for a high school summer band concert. I crossed the street and stopped at the war memorial. It was a large block of white stone with plaques for overseas conflicts in which American boys had fought and died. There were plaques for World War I, World War II, Korea, Vietnam, and Desert Storm. We had run a story on the new plaque in the Sunday issue of the Banner. I had been surprised at how quickly the City Council had officially recognized Desert Storm, and I was pleased for Tag.

Next to the war memorial was a granite marker with a bronze plaque that read: "Massacre Site." Back in 1862 a dozen men were killed here by a group of border renegades. The men were just farmers and shopkeepers, rounded up for no other reason than that the renegades were drunk and wanted something to do. As I stood there on the town square now, with the music of the high school band in the background, it seemed hardly possible that twelve men had been shot here, had gazed at these same old brick buildings as they were pushed into a circle and the muskets opened fire. What would I have been thinking if I had been one of those men? I wondered. Did they have time to be afraid? Did it seem unreal to them? Had they received any premonition from God that this would be their last day on earth? Had Mark Wayland received any premonition from God? Did he believe in God?

The sound of shoe heels on gravel caused me to look up. An old man in a gray cloth cap was coming slowly up the sidewalk. His blue overalls were worn and faded, and his flannel shirt was buttoned neatly at the collar. He carried a brown paper sack in his right hand.

"Evening, Donny," the old man said.

"Hello, Mr. Cully," I said. Mr. Cully was a retired railroader, just as Grandfather Graham had been. He had often brought us a sack of tomatoes or string beans from his garden. As a boy I had been fascinated by his mutilated hand and horrified at the image of having fingers severed while uncoupling freight cars. I remembered gazing up at those eyes, ice blue and direct, from the front porch as he and my grandfather talked about railroading.

"Going to the concert?" I asked.

The old man clutched the brown paper sack in his hands. "I was just on my way up to the tracks. The express should be going by in a few minutes."

"Does it stop?" I didn't remember any trains ever stopping at the Sixth Street crossing except when work was being done on the rails, or when a freight car was being disconnected.

"No," Mr. Cully said and smiled shyly. "I just like to watch it go past. Reminds me of the old days."

On a sudden whim I asked, "Mind if I join you?" I was tired of thinking about balance and metaphorical actions and the problems of others. I wanted to get away from it all and to pass a few moments in simplicity.

Mr. Cully looked surprised. "Not at all, Donny. Glad to have the company."

It was three blocks past the granary to the crossing. As we walked along the street, I thought of all the times I had stood on the corner of Highland Avenue with my mother and watched as the 2:15 to St. Louis had sped through. First came the blur of passenger cars, the coaches painted maroon because they belonged to the Pennsylvania Railroad, and then the white handkerchief being waved from a platform window—that was Grandpa Graham signaling that he was scheduled to make a round-about in St. Louis and would be home for dinner. In my mind I could see the waving handkerchief now as we approached the crossing, and could feel the joy it had given me to know my grandfather would be coming home later that evening.

I could remember walking along the curb until I found enough pebbles to make an army and then rounding the house and playing with the pebbles in the gray, sooty dust of my grandparents' back yard. The dirt had not always been so sooty, Uncle Walter had told me. The black soot had come from the trains that had passed every day on the twelve tracks just down the block, trains speeding along from mysterious destinations with passengers who glanced quickly out the windows and then returned to whatever they were reading—or talking about with other passengers who were equally important and mysterious. The trains had passed and the soot from their smokestacks had blown back over the cars and then swirled into the air and had settled over the town. By the time I was born, all the engines were diesel, but the speeding trains still lifted soot from the tracks into the air, and I had felt it becoming a part of me as I grew, marking me from my birthplace. This was not an unpleasant thing.

Mr. Cully gazed up the street. "Eden Springs ain't like it used to be," he said, shaking his head sadly. "Place has gone to pot. Nobody takes care of anything anymore. During the depression we didn't have anything, but we took care of what we had. Nobody does that now."

"It's a shame," I said.

"Used to be twelve tracks here—a real working yard," Mr. Cully said with a sweep of his mutilated hand. "Not anymore. Two tracks now. Nothing but a few trains passing during the day. Mostly freight."

I nodded. "Even before my grandfather retired, he was worried about the railroad."

"I know," Mr. Cully said. "I said it too. We all said it."

A gray stone wall ran along the sidewalk beside the tracks. Mr. Cully stopped here. He sat down on the cool, moss-covered stones and let out a sigh.

"Come up here nearly every evening when the weather's warm," he said, gazing up the track. "It's a nice break from the house."

I sat down beside him.

Mr. Cully opened his sack and removed a Styrofoam cup of coffee. "It's part of my routine," he said, pulling a packet of sugar from his shirt pocket. He tore open the packet with his teeth and sprinkled it into the coffee. "I get a cup at the Gas Mart every time I come down to the tracks."

"That's a good idea," I said.

"Want some?" he asked, offering me the cup.

"No thanks."

Mr. Cully's eyes brightened expectantly, and he looked up the track. "Here she comes."

"The train?"

"Yes."

The signal arms were coming down on both sides of the crossing, and the lights began to flash. A moment later the clanging alarm began to sound.

"I always wanted to be a railroader when I was a boy," I admitted. "It seemed like a good life."

"I liked it," Mr. Cully said.

The ground began to vibrate with the motion of the train. It came in a heavy, pulsating rush of rolling steel on steel until the engine was beside us, and the engineer reached out a gloved hand and waved to Mr. Cully.

"A friend of yours?" I shouted.

Mr. Cully nodded, amused.

There were five passenger cars, and I gazed at each of them, half expecting to see an elderly man in a black conductor's uniform standing on one of the platforms and waving at me. There was no caboose, and the train flashed by in a long, clicking moment, and then we were gazing at the receding last coach as the vibrating diminished. We watched without talking until the train had gone up the track and disappeared around a curve near the tool-and-die factory.

"Bill's going to retire next year," Mr. Cully said. "Been railroading a long time."

"Who's that?" I asked.

"The engineer."

I started to get up from the wall.

"I usually sit here for a while after the train has passed," Mr. Cully said. "No point in hurrying home."

I gazed at the white stubble of beard on the old man's face and at his white mustache. "Do you like to fish?" I asked. A thought had occurred to me.

Mr. Cully focused his eyes on the track ahead thoughtfully. "Yes, I do," he said. "But I haven't been for a long time."

"Would you like to go sometime?" I asked. "There's some nice bluegill out at Wingert Lake."

Mr. Cully pushed the gray hat back on his head. "When?"

"Saturday morning."

A shy smile began to form at the corners of his mouth.

"Sure," he said at last. "I'd like that."

Thirteen

~

A subtle yet pervasive force spread through Eden Springs in the weeks following the F16 crash. This was the dark underside of life in a small town—the ugliness of people when they turn against you. At parties and on the street everyone discussed the crash. Who was to blame? they debated. Who had done such an irresponsible thing? At the same time, a growing resentment and bitterness had attached itself to the airmen who might have been involved. I didn't know how serious it had become until I called Tag one afternoon. When his mother answered, I could tell that she was upset.

"Mrs. Taggart," I said, "is everything all right?"

She took a moment to compose herself. "Yes, Donny," she said at last. "I'm so glad you called." Then she added, in almost a whisper: "Tag needs a friend."

"He has Sylvie," I reminded her.

"Yes," she sniffled. "He does. She's such a fine girl too."

When Tag came on the line, his tone was somber. I explained that Anne and I were going out for dinner and asked if he and Sylvie would like to join us.

"I can't," he said. "It wouldn't be any fun."

"What do you mean?"

"C'mon, Donny," he said, without further explanation.

"Then how about going for a drive?"

"Where?"

"I don't know—someplace out of town. Maybe that old barbecue restaurant on Route J."

"Why?"

"Why?" I asked in return. "To spend some time together."

"Listen, Donny," Tag said. "Maybe we should talk."

We discussed several places to meet and finally decided on the bluff overlooking the strip mine. This was across the river. We had ridden out there frequently as teenagers to shoot cans and to brag about where we were going in life. Neither of us felt like bragging now, however. His car was parked by the gravel edge of the bluff when I arrived. He must have left the moment I hung up the telephone.

"How's it going?" I asked.

Tag picked up a rock and tossed it into the strip mine. It made a gray puff of dust when it struck bottom.

"I've always tried to be a good airman," he commented. "The Air Force is important to me. I've seen things and done things that . . ."

He let this trail off.

"What did you want to talk about?" I asked.

Tag picked up another rock. "I know the timing couldn't be worse," he began, "but I'm thinking about asking Sylvie to marry me."

He turned and gazed at me questioningly.

A series of cliché responses came quickly to my mind. I wanted to say, "You're kidding," or "You're joking," or "You're out of your mind." But I could only shake my head in surprise.

"Aren't there some things you need to resolve first?" I asked.

Tag shrugged. "There will always be things, Donny. Always. Haven't you learned that by now?"

I picked up a stone. "Do you want my advice?"

Tag ran a hand over his short-clipped hair. "No. I wanted to tell you so you wouldn't hear it from someone else. I know how people have been talking lately."

"It's a shame," I said.

A hawk flew up from the direction of the river and began to circle over a field on the south side of the mine. It circled widely for several minutes and then went into a dive. After a moment it flapped into the air again, but if it had caught anything, I couldn't see.

"Have you talked to Sylvie?" I asked.

"About getting married?"

How could I word this? I wondered. I wanted to ask him why he wanted to marry my cousin, but that was obvious—or at least the superficial reasons were obvious—for attraction sometimes comes from a depth that is beyond our understanding.

"She's an innocent girl," I offered. "In some ways, a really sweet girl."

I hesitated after saying this.

"I know she is," Tag replied.

"But she hasn't talked to you?"

His eyes grew dark. "What are you getting at, Donny?"

"She had an experience . . ." I began, but I couldn't continue. Gazing at the ground, I shook my head. I could feel my lower lip beginning to tighten.

"An experience?"

"She'll have to tell you."

Tag looked hard at me for a minute, trying to understand, and then kicked at the rocky edge of the bluff. "I'm still going to ask her."

My mind was beginning to clear. There was something else I wanted to know.

"Did you have any trouble working on Mark Wayland's jet after you learned he had dated Sylvie?" I asked.

Tag's eyes flashed angrily, and I suddenly saw him from a new perspective. For the first time, I wondered if I could take him in a fight.

"What does that mean?"

I tossed a flat piece of sandstone into the air. It floated above the trees for a moment and then began its quick descent into the pit. I thought of a jet making that same descent.

"Who left the rag in the engine, Tag?" I asked quietly. "Was it you?"

His jaw tightened, and I backed subtly away from the edge of the bluff.

"What would you do if I said yes?" he snapped. "Would you tell?"

I had to think about that for a moment.

"No," I said, finally. "I'm only asking as your friend."

"As my friend," he said angrily. "Wouldn't you feel the need to tell someone. Maybe Anne, or Melissa, or . . . Sylvie?"

"No."

"I'm sorry, Donny, but I can't help you," he said bitterly. "Well, I could . . . but then I'd have to kill you."

He gave a short, unconvincing laugh.

I headed toward my Trooper.

"You can't even see it, can you?" he shouted. "This sudden need to know?"

"What?" I asked, becoming angry myself.

"You don't want me to marry your cousin. Isn't that it? You don't want me to marry Sylvie, so you're looking for excuses."

"That's not it at all," I said. "I'm trying to find out who you are."

I walked back to him and looked him in the eyes. "Who are you?" I demanded. "What happened to my friend?"

Tag turned his face away from me and didn't say anything for a long time. When he looked up again, the anger was gone. "He's lost," he said, almost in a whisper. "Lost . . . back there in the desert." He gazed off in the direction of the strip mine as if he were seeing a horizon of sand dunes and runways and aircraft hangars.

"Why?" I asked. "What happened?"

"I should have told you before," he said. "I tried a couple of times, but it was too hard. Sometimes I can talk about it. Maybe today . . ."

He began to trail off again, so I pressed him.

"What happened?"

I don't know if we are ever prepared for the revelations of friends. As we move about in this world, we imagine that others share our experiences, face similar problems, cry over the same tragedies. So it is a shock when we discover that someone we have known for years has encountered life in a totally different reality, has spun off in a different direction from our own. Tag's experiences in the war were something I could never share, but I didn't assume that it would also change who he was on the inside. I realize now that was very naive of me. It would have altered everything if I had known. But I didn't, so I plodded on like an insensitive fool, pressing forcefully against a wound. I did not feel the pain and therefore was not aware it existed.

Tag dropped onto the rocks with his legs dangling over the edge of the pit. For a moment I had a sudden fear that he was going to jump, and I thought about how I would grab his shirt if I saw him beginning to slide. But he had no intention of falling, at least not in a physical sense.

"Do you really believe there is a God, Donny?" he asked absently, gazing at the sunlight fading behind the trees.

There was an urgency to his question that betrayed more than curiosity. I sensed that he needed some reassurance, to know for sure.

"Yes," I said, with utter conviction. "I've always believed. That hasn't been the problem."

"But when someone believes and dies," he continued. "They go to heaven, right? It's a sure thing?"

"Jesus says He is the resurrection and the life," I replied, and then quoted: "He who believes in me will live even if he dies."

Tag sighed deeply.

"So, do you want to tell me?" I asked.

"Yeah," he said. He did not look at me as he talked, but gazed out at the strip mine as if the person he was speaking to hung somewhere out there in the fading twilight.

Fourteen

~

All the boys who joined the Air Force from Eden Springs received their basic training at Lackland AFB in San Antonio, Texas. (In fact, I had driven Tag to the station myself three years ago so he could catch his bus to Texas. He had been excited and nervous standing there in the doorway with his bag.) At Lackland, Tag had met another recruit named Ted Armbruster. Armbruster, or "Bear" as he was known to his friends, was from Cheyenne, Wyoming. He was a tall blond kid with an easy grin and a flair for picking up girls—although once they had been introduced to Tag they usually lost interest in Bear. Armbruster was a thinking man, an articulate guy who was generally one step ahead of Tag intellectually. But he was not as worldly as Tag, nor did he have the intensity. Perhaps because of their differences, Tag and Bear became close friends and spent their free time during basic hanging around the clubs together. They both were trained for aircraft maintenance at Sheppard AFB in Wichita Falls and then were sent to Luke AFB in Phoenix for additional F16 training. At this point they could easily have been sent to bases halfway around the world from each other, but instead they were assigned to the F16 squadron at Adana, Turkey.

(Perhaps this was not such a coincidence after all, for things were beginning to heat up in the Gulf.)

As Tag mentioned this, I remembered a postcard he had sent me from Turkey. I had thought about the apostle Paul and his journeys through Ephesus, the town that was said to have been the last home of Mary. It seemed that Tag's military service was taking on a biblical theme.

"I pray that the eyes of your heart may be enlightened," I could hear Paul saying, "so that you will know what is the hope of His calling."

After the Iraqi invasion of Kuwait, Tag and Bear's squadron was deployed to Riyadh and the preparations for war began.

Tag stopped talking after he had explained this and put his hands over his eyes.

"I never took it that seriously," he said. "I thought we were invincible. Some of the pilots were scared. You could see it in their eyes. But I didn't really think anyone would get hurt. I didn't really believe there would be twenty percent casualties on the first mission. It seemed too improbable . . ."

I gazed at the darkening line of trees across the mine. "I've never been in a war," I offered. "But it seems to me that you could never really imagine war, either. It's like a break in reality—a rip where all logical and reasonable thinking ceases to exist. Only when it's over and the dead have been quietly buried does reality begin again."

Tag nodded. The base had been warned of Scud missile attacks, he continued, but up to that point nothing had happened. Then on the evening of January 19, while he and Bear were inspecting a jet that had just returned from a mission and was still on the ramp, the siren had gone off. It began in a low growl that intensified into a nerve-wracking wail.

Tag paused here as if to gather his thoughts. I wondered if it was important for him to get the details as exact as possible, so that the story did not alter over time into something unreal.

"I wanted to run for cover," Tag explained. "We had built makeshift bunkers along the ramp and piled them with sandbags. They would never withstand a direct hit, but they were better than being in the open. But Bear said we couldn't leave the F16 just sitting on the ramp. We had to back it into the hangar."

The "alarm red" siren had been wailing for about sixty seconds, he said.

"I said there wasn't time, but Bear said we had at least five minutes," Tag continued. "So we ran into the hangar and got the tractor."

The jets were backed into the hangars by a small tractor that attached to the front wheel of the aircraft. Usually there was an airman on either side of the jet to make sure that the wings were clear. The tractor pushed the jet into the hangar, much like a truck pushed a boat trailer down to a landing.

The base had now been in "alarm red" status for three minutes.

"We had the tractor hooked up to the F16, and Bear was backing it in," Tag offered. "I was walking the wing on the near side."

Tag suddenly put both hands up to his shoulders and began to massage his neck.

"That's when . . ."

I waited, feeling that it was impossible to say anything.

"That's when the first Scud hit," Tag muttered. "It hit on the south side of the base by the landing repair building. I told Bear to forget it, that we should take cover, but he shouted that we were almost in the hangar. So we kept the jet moving, and then Bear stopped and told me to run around to the far side and check the wing. He was getting close."

Tag hesitated and gazed out to the darkness of the strip mine. I could tell that he wasn't just telling the story of the attack but was reliving it. I could only imagine what he was seeing and hearing as we stood in the darkening silence of the countryside.

"We got the F16 into the hangar, and then Bear jumped off the tractor and we began to close the doors," Tag sighed. "That's when the second Scud hit. The explosion was about two hundred yards from our ramp. I was on the far side of the hangar door, so it only knocked me down. But Bear . . ."

Tag's voice trembled. "Bear . . ."

"He didn't make it?" I asked.

Tag shook his head slowly. "That's why I've got to know he's in heaven. Otherwise, I couldn't live with myself. I feel like I went up with him—like I've lost a part of myself."

"He's in heaven," I said. "If he believed, then he's in heaven. I can promise you that."

Tag nodded and wiped his face on his shirt sleeve. It was almost dark now, and I could see fireflies skimming through the tall grass.

We sat there for about fifteen minutes without talking. I had no idea what to say.

Finally I glanced at my watch.

"We'd better be going," I urged. "I promised Anne I'd take her out tonight."

"Sure," Tag said. His voice sounded tired.

"I'm really sorry, Tag."

He picked up a stone and tossed it into the darkening pit. "We're all sorry, Donny. The question is, how far does sorry go? When is remorse ever enough?"

"Enough for what?"

"To change things."

"Well," I said and considered for a moment. "Never."

Tag laughed bitterly. "So there you have it. You're sorry so much that it hurts, so that you can barely stand it, and then you realize even that degree of pain means nothing. It's never enough. We can't change anything."

"The only way I've ever found to change anything is through prayer," I offered.

"Prayer," Tag muttered. "I tried that with my father. It didn't help."

"With your father?"

Tag looked at me. "Don't you remember Melissa saying that her father had seen me climbing up the wisteria vine to my window at daybreak?"

I nodded.

"Where did you think I'd been?"

I shrugged. "I don't know. Out partying, I guess."

"I figured you thought that. But I wasn't." He shook his head in disbelief. "You want to know where I was?"

"Sure."

"I was sitting on the steps of the First Assembly Church of Eden Springs—praying that my father wouldn't die of leukemia."

"I had no idea."

"I wanted to be as close as I could get to God, so maybe He would hear my prayer. So I sat on the steps all night. Can you believe that?"

"I've often felt that way," I replied. "I understand."

"But it didn't work," Tag said. "I did it three, maybe four times. Then I stopped praying."

"Just because you didn't get the response you wanted doesn't mean God didn't hear your prayer."

"Maybe," Tag said. "But now I've got to know about Bear. If he's okay, then I can ease off the pain."

"I told you," I said.

Tag nodded. "Right."

The stars were bright over our heads now. It was dangerous to be so close to the edge of the mine.

"So . . ." I said and waited.

Tag continued to sit with his legs dangling over the edge. "I think I'll stay here for a while, Donny."

"Do you want me to stay, too?" I asked.

"No. I'll be all right."

I stood up. "Thanks for letting me know about Sylvie. Have you asked her yet?"

Tag looked up at the night sky.

"We've kind of hinted around at it—you know how that is," he said. "I haven't officially popped the question."

"So what's the plan?"

"I was thinking about Sunday. She wants me to go to church with her and Melissa. I thought maybe afterwards we could drive out somewhere quiet—away from Eden Springs," he added quickly. "And I'd ask her then."

"Sounds good."

"I wanted to ask her tomorrow, but I have an appointment at the VA hospital. I'll be back on Saturday."

"Nothing serious, I hope."

"I've just been feeling weird lately."

"Is that what was bothering you that day at the skeet club?"

Tag thought about this for a moment and then shook his head. "No, that was something else."

"But you're okay?"

He shrugged. "It comes and goes. Not so often lately."

"Because of Sylvie?"

Tag smiled. "Yeah, probably because of Sylvie."

"When does the board make its decision?" I asked.

"In a few weeks."

"It must be terrible."

Tag shook his head. "It's nothing, Donny. Nothing at all."

Fifteen

~

The telephone rang as I was seated at my desk writing a quick story on a fire at the antique shop on Harrison Street. The fire had started at the back of the store and had been put out by the Eden Springs Fire Department, but not before several pieces of furniture were destroyed. Oddly enough one of the pieces was an old oak desk that had belonged to Grandfather Graham. I had been meaning for months to pick up that desk, but there was really no place to put it in my small apartment. Now it was lost. I thought about old pieces of furniture and how there might be a feature story in tracking down some of these pieces in Eden Springs and writing about their histories. It wasn't really my kind of story, but I could keep it for a slow day. The phone rang, and I picked it up. The voice on the other end of the line was unfamiliar.

"Mr. Foster?" the man asked.

"Yes," I replied.

"This is Captain Higdon. I work for the judge advocate general's office, and I'm investigating the F16 crash. I wondered if I could ask you a few questions."

"I've already given a statement," I said. "It should be in the SIB report."

"I know that," Higdon said, with the implication that he had already read it. "I wanted to ask you a few background questions."

I glanced at my watch. "I'm rather busy right now, Captain Higdon. Could we discuss this later?"

"Of course," he said politely.

"I should be off work at six."

"I'd like to make this informal," Higdon said. "Is there somewhere we could meet for a few minutes?"

I had to think for a moment. I had no intention of driving out to the base. Neither did I want some JAG officer in my apartment. A public place would be better.

"How about Darby's?" I asked. This was a popular restaurant on Ash Street. Many Air Force people went there in the evenings.

"Six thirty?"

"I'll be waiting at the hostess stand," I said, and then added sarcastically: "I'll be the one with the pencil behind my ear."

"I know what you look like," he said and hung up.

As I dropped the receiver slowly into its cradle, a feeling of uneasiness swept over me.

Actually, I hadn't been in Darby's for a long time. It wasn't the kind of restaurant Anne appreciated—she didn't like crowds. And I was on a limited budget. It was an old-fashioned place in one of the oldest buildings in town—existing since the massacre in 1862. Inside was a long wooden bar with a brass rail, about twenty tables with checkered cloths, and a shuffleboard game against the wall. I arrived early, waited for a few minutes near the entrance, and then walked over to the bar.

"Hello, Donny," the bartender called to me. "How've you been?"

"Okay, Rico," I said. "How's the swing?"

"I can still hit it out of the park," he said and grinned.

"I heard you beat the team from the tool-and-die factory last weekend."

"That was two weeks ago."

"Right."

"I think their pitcher was playing with a bad arm. He had nothing on the ball."

I smiled and looked around the restaurant. It was still early, and only a few tables were occupied.

"So how's business?"

Rico shrugged. "A little slow since the crash. Maybe nobody wants to make a mistake."

"I guess so."

Rico reached for a glass, filled it with club soda, tossed in a wedge of lime, and set it on a bar pad in front of me.

"Working on a story?" he asked while filling a container with sliced oranges.

I shook my head. "I'm just waiting for someone."

"Try the cheese," he urged, setting a brown crock of cheddar cheese and a bowl of crackers in front of me. "It's pretty good."

A small knife with a wooden handle was stuck in the cheese. I scooped some out and spread it on a cracker.

"You're right," I said. "This is good."

I had just stuffed another cracker into my mouth when someone beside me said, "Mr. Foster?"

I turned to see a gray-haired man in a dress-blue uniform. He had a pleasant smile, which masked the intensity of an analytical gaze. I could perceive a core of inner toughness behind his wire-rimmed glasses.

I nodded, trying to swallow the dry bits of cracker and cheese. Great first impression, I thought, but then grew irritated with myself. What did I care about making an impression on this guy? He was a JAG officer in an investigation in which my friend was involved. Unless he was here to help Tag, this was a waste of time.

"Yes," I said, taking a sip of club soda. "Have a seat."

Higdon's jaw tightened, and he rubbed the corners of his mouth. "Some of the questions I need to ask you are of a personal nature, Mr. Foster," he stated, glancing at the bartender. "Wouldn't you rather sit at a table?"

I had no intention of sitting across from Higdon for half an hour while he asked me questions and studied my responses. If we couldn't sit at the bar, then I would prefer to be moving.

"How about a game of shuffleboard?" I asked. "We can talk while we play."

Higdon glanced at the shuffleboard table against the wall. The dining tables in that area were empty.

"All right," he said and nodded without enthusiasm.

It was a funny thing about shuffleboard. I really liked the game. I suppose it was because I had fond memories of watching my father play at the tavern on Cherry Avenue. I wasn't supposed to be in a tavern when I was nine years old, but sometimes when we were out running errands my father would say, "Donny, I'll just run in and get something to settle my stomach." Then he would pull the green and white Oldsmobile over to the curb. The Cherry Avenue Tavern. It was the epitome of everything I later despised in life: the thick odor of whiskey, the flushed faces of patrons gazing at me from bar stools, the red and blue neon sign that blinked out a lonely staccato in the window, the impression of lost and worthless lives, a harbor for the broken and failed. My father would order a beer in a longneck bottle for himself and a soda with a maraschino cherry for me, and then we would go over to the shuffleboard table. My father was good, and I can remember the silver metal disks swishing down the board through the thin filament of sawdust—just enough to make the disks really float—and then seeming to come to an almost unbelievable halt at the end of the board without dropping over the edge. My father could do that. He could make those shuffleboard disks hang on the edge and at the corners, too. He would take a swig of beer, wink at me, lean far over the table, and let the disk slip from his fingers.

"Watch this, Donny," he would say.

And I would respond, "I'm watching, Dad."

But what was I watching? Cirrhosis of the liver, high blood pressure, a heart attack at fifty, a mother who worked a full time job and took care of a family until . . .

I picked up one of the shuffleboard discs and skimmed it down the long wooden table.

Higdon picked up a disk and turned it over in his hand thoughtfully.

"Are you new here?" I asked.

"I was brought in from Lackland for the investigation."

He slid the disk down the board, and it went off the edge before crossing the line. A rookie, I told myself.

"Prosecution or defense?"

Higdon looked suspiciously around the restaurant. "Neither. This isn't a court-martial. I'm only trying to find out what went wrong."

"So you don't know?"

He looked at me. "I know you're a reporter for the Banner. Is this on the record?"

I laughed. "No."

He wiped the corners of his mouth again. "We know someone left a rag in the engine after Captain Wayland's morning flight on July 9. Several members of the ground crew had access to the aircraft that day and the following morning."

"Do you have a list?"

"Of course."

"But you haven't pinned the blame on anyone yet?"

Higdon shook his head and slid another disc down the table. "I'm much better at tennis."

"I don't play tennis," I said. "It takes up too much time."

"Time for what?" Higdon asked.

I had to smile. "I've been wondering that myself."

The minutes ticked by, and I felt myself beginning to let down my guard. Higdon had taken off his jacket, folded it neatly and placed it over the back of a chair. He struck me as being a nice guy.

"Do you have any kids?" I asked.

"Two girls. And you?"

"I'm not married," I said, though I knew this wasn't an answer.

Higdon straightened up from the board and looked at me. "Shall we get down to the questions?" he asked.

I nodded reluctantly.

"I'm not trying to put you on the spot, Mr. Foster," he said. "I simply need to know some background on Airman Taggart. I understand you're a friend of his?"

I nodded again.

"I've heard that Airman Taggart has acted oddly at times while off duty. Could you confirm this?"

"In what way?" I asked.

Higdon took off his glasses and pulled a handkerchief from his pocket. "Moments of losing touch—anxiety?"

I took a deep breath. "I've seen him do that," I admitted. "Is it from the Scud missile attack? When you lose a friend . . ."

"He was lucky to have survived."

"So you know about that?" I asked.

"It's in his file. He's up for the Bronze Star."

"Really," I said. "A Bronze Star. I didn't know that."

"He didn't tell you about it?"

"No."

"Well," Higdon said and put on his glasses. "Some servicemen don't like to talk about their wartime experiences."

"Especially if they were bad ones," I commented.

Higdon nodded in agreement. "Right."

"And you think maybe this trauma or whatever caused Tag to leave a rag in the engine?"

Higdon shook his head. "I'm not making any assumptions, Mr. Foster. I'm only trying to find out what happened"

Leaning over the board, he slid a disc along the right edge of the table and knocked one of my pieces off.

"You're getting better."

"I'm from Oklahoma," Higdon said, as if that were an explanation.

Sixteen

~

For a time I believed my life was filled with a variety of strangely fortuitous coincidences. For example, it was strange that I had met Anne through a mutual friend whom neither of us had seen since. And that I would meet Ed Thomas on a commuter flight and he would offer me a job on the newspaper. Or that I would take Tag to a dance where he would meet the woman he wished to marry. I believed these coincidences were unexplained, but now I realize this was the subtle yet direct influence of divine providence in our lives. So it seems ridiculous to look back on the events of that summer and fall and to imagine that they could have transpired in any other way. But then personal loyalty and integrity were involved, and these are traits that must be taken into consideration.

When Tag returned to Eden Springs from the VA hospital, he was thinner. His skin, which usually tanned easily, had grown pale, and he kept more to himself. I wanted to call him but refrained for a few days, thinking that the timing was not right. He had been given two weeks sick leave and was recuperating. What could I have said or done anyway? Then one evening after work, I drove past his house. It was a warm evening, and the

moon was up. Crickets chirped on the lawn. As I came up
the walk, I saw Tag and Sylvie sitting peacefully in an
Adirondack chair on the porch. Tag's arm was around
Sylvie's shoulders, and she was pressed against him. Her
eyes, shining in the yellow light from the two door lamps,
gazed at me with more tenderness than I had ever known.
So, I thought to myself, Tag has asked her. He has asked
her, and she has obviously said yes. And it has just
happened, too.

I could tell that from the expression on her face. It
was as if her mouth and eyes had been freshly painted by
Renoir. I was wrong to have ever doubted, I told myself.
Tag is good for her, and she . . . well, I had always taken
for granted that any man who married my cousin was
blessed in more ways than he could imagine. I also
realized that my timing couldn't have been more
inappropriate.

"I'm sorry," I said. "I just thought I'd drop by and see
how you were doing."

Tag smiled weakly, but with an air of total acceptance.
The French have an expression, *Il est bien dans sa peau,*
which is difficult to translate but generally means that a
man is comfortable or at peace with himself. This is how
Tag looked as he sat beside Sylvie. And I thought: So this
is how a man appears when the struggle is over and he
has found himself in a safe harbor and away from the
storms of life. Can anything hurt him now? Does it matter
what happens with the crash investigation? And I felt
suddenly envious; it swept through me like an ache. I
wasn't envious of his relationship with Sylvie but of his
ability to be *at peace.* I cared for Anne, but I had never felt
that way, known that bond of affection, that calm feeling
of assurance. And I knew it was my fault. Sometime in

my past, something had hardened within me, and now I found it difficult to retain affection. It was much easier to stay aloof.

"Tag has just asked me to marry him," Sylvie explained, reaching out for my hand.

"That's great," I said, feeling the coolness of her fingers. "I'm really happy for you."

Sitting in my apartment that night and gazing across the square from the sycamore trees and the war memorial to the massacre plaque, I thought about the direction my life had taken since I had joined the Banner staff. We were only here for so short a time, I told myself. So short a time. A day was like a thousand years to the Almighty, and a thousand years like a day. I had come to think of a lifetime as eighty years. We were on this earth for a mere eighty years, and where was I now? What day was I living at this moment? People had died right down there; men who had wanted to live, who probably had wives, children, a belief in God. Had they wasted it? Had the soldiers whose names were engraved on the war memorial wasted it? Had I wasted it? I felt that way now. I felt as if the life I had built for myself in Eden Springs had fallen around me like dust. "It's time to stop running, Donny," I muttered. Tag had stopped running.

That wasn't really true, I told myself. Tag had never been running. I think he knew that, and he also knew that I always had been. He had never said anything, though, and I appreciated this demonstration of his friendship.

There was a knock on my door. I gazed out the window a moment longer and then crossed the room.

"I think there's something wrong with your phone," Anne said, smiling up at me. "I tried calling several times."

"No," I said distantly. "It's unplugged."

She looked at me in confusion. There were so many ramifications to the fact that I had disconnected the phone. Hadn't I known that she would call when she got off work? she asked.

"Yes," I said, and could see the hurt in her eyes.

It was still dark when I pulled up to Mr. Cully's house. The early morning streets were quiet, and my Trooper rolled over the crackling pods of plane trees and the gravel. His house was at the end of a dead-end street. It was perhaps the smallest house I had ever seen—just a shack with a tar-paper roof and screened porch. I thought about how the material possessions of our lives seem to diminish as we diminish, to grow smaller and less complicated as we become smaller and less complicated. Here was an old man who had lived his life and was now waiting patiently for the final diminishment. Above my head I could hear the sparrows beginning their morning song in the oak trees that surrounded the shack. I wondered if Mr. Cully ever awakened from sleep in the morning and forgot for an instant that he was old, that his body had nearly relinquished the fight. If that were true, then who was he when he opened his eyes in the gray light and heard the birds singing outside his window? Was he a boy? A young man? Or was he just himself, unencumbered by the boundaries of time and age?

The screen door squeaked open.

"Be with you in a minute, Donny," he said. "Just finishing my coffee."

"I brought the thermos," I said. "There's plenty for both of us."

"Okay, then," he said and smiled. He had put on a clean shirt and combed his hair back with water. His face was unshaven and still retained the gray stubble. "I'll get my tackle box."

I had never been inside Mr. Cully's house, though I had waited in the doorway long enough to see inside. Off to the left was a small room with a couch and a card table. An old Indian blanket and a pillow were draped over the couch, so I assumed this served as Mr. Cully's living room and sleeping room. Also, there was a small air conditioner in the window. The room on the right was empty except for a table saw and piles of wood shavings. It was an old man's house, dirty and unkempt and primitive. Would I be living like this in fifty years? I asked myself. Did I have a choice? It was the possibility of a choice that bothered me. The inevitable was much easier to accept.

Mr. Cully held up a box. "I got us some crickets," he said. "Better than the worms we used last time."

This was our second trip to Wingert Lake. The first time Mr. Cully had caught three bluegills and I had caught two. I had enjoyed the peacefulness of the lake at dawn and the pleasant, easy conversation.

"I picked up some donuts, too," I added as Mr. Cully set his tackle in the back of the Trooper.

"Well," he said and grinned. "This is a real picnic."

We headed east out of town through the dark fields and woods. The sky was brightening as we turned off the paved road onto a gravel track that wound around the lake to a clearing where we could put in the canoe.

"It's a fine morning," Mr. Cully said as he gazed at the lapping water.

I hoped he was right. I wanted it to be a fine morning on the lake, because I had been up all night thinking about Anne. Sometimes we do things that, even at the moment of doing them, we cannot believe are really happening. I loved Anne, and I never wanted to hurt her. Now, as I unstrapped the canoe from the top of the Trooper, I thought about the softness of her hair and how it felt so reassuring against my cheek, the timid determination of her mouth, the dark, competent eyes that searched for acceptance, the comforting lilt of her voice that promised happiness, always happiness and joy. That was her gift to me, because I lacked those things. Happiness was something I borrowed from others, like a fine wine that I could only share in their presence. But there came a time when even the possibility of a fine wine was unbearable.

"Look," I said and pointed.

A blue heron was skimming across the lake. It floated effortlessly above the water.

"I've seen him out here before," Mr. Cully said. "I believe he's the only one."

We carried the canoe down to the water's edge and loaded it with the tackle and bait. The soft, green water felt cold around my ankles as I waded out a few steps and then got into the canoe. Mr. Cully climbed in behind me.

"Ready?" I asked.

He nodded.

I dipped the paddle into the water and pushed, and the canoe slipped away from the shore.

"Let's try that same cove we fished last time," I called back over my shoulder.

Mr. Cully nodded in agreement.

We paddled into the northern cove of Wingert Lake, and I turned around to the bait box. Mr. Cully had already taken out a cricket and was slipping the hook under the jaw and down into the abdomen. I opened the small hole of the box, and a cricket stuck out its head. I waited until the insect had stepped out with both its front feet and antennae and then grabbed it between my fingers.

Mr. Cully smiled mischievously.

"Here goes," he said, casting his line into the water.

"I'll try over here," I said.

We fished for thirty minutes without talking. Mr. Cully caught a small bluegill and tossed it back in the water. The sky was light now, and I could see across the lake. The air smelled dry, and I imagined it was going to be another hot day.

"Coffee?" I asked.

"I brought my own cup," Mr. Cully said and pulled a cracked coffee mug from his fishing bag.

I unscrewed the thermos and poured the coffee.

"Still hot," he commented and smiled appreciatively.

"It's a good thermos," I said. "How about a donut?"

Mr. Cully reeled in his line a little. "Thanks."

I handed him the bag, and he took a donut. They were simple cake donuts, but they had been made that morning. He took a bite and looked around the lake.

"I remember when this lake was built," he said. "Just after the war. Weren't nothing out here then but a few old shacks."

"That was before my time," I offered.

"Yep," he said, gazing at his line. "That was a long time ago."

I felt a tug on my line and began to reel in.

"You got one," Mr. Cully said. "Just keep it steady. I'll get the net."

I reeled in steadily until I saw the silver curve of a fish cut through the water below my line.

"That's fine," Mr. Cully coached. "A little more."

I shifted the rod to the right and reeled in as Mr. Cully dipped the net into the water.

When he lifted the net, I could see a large bluegill.

"Want me to get the hook?" he asked.

"I'll get it."

I slipped my hand down along the gills of the fish and grasped it firmly. Then I removed the hook from the jaw.

"Good catch," Mr. Cully said. "That's a keeper."

I dropped the fish into the bucket and reached for another cricket.

"Were you in the war, Mr. Cully?" I asked, thinking about Tag's experience.

"Sure," he answered. "Everyone was."

"I thought—with your hand . . ."

Mr. Cully held up his mutilated hand. "No," he replied. "I got this after."

"Were you in the Army?"

The old man straightened his shoulders proudly. "Marines."

"Marines," I said. "Then you must have been in the Pacific."

He nodded. "Iwo Jima."

"What was it like? I've heard stories . . ."

The pride drained quickly from his face, and his back slumped. A distant look came into his eyes.

"I never talk about it," he said.

"I only thought . . ." But even as I spoke, I realized that I had seen that look, that expression in the eyes before.

"I *never* talk about it," Mr. Cully said again, more firmly.

"I'm sorry," I said.

He gazed at his line. "It's not like these boys now who dress up and go out and pretend to be soldiers."

"You mean Desert Storm?"

Mr. Cully waved his mutilated hand at me. "No, no. These militia boys. You know, like that Stan Drussell and his group. Them weekend soldiers."

It took a minute for this information to register.

"Stan Drussell is in a militia unit?"

Mr. Cully nodded. "They like it to be kind of hush-hush, you know, but I seen 'em all dressed up. You can't hide nothing in a town this small. I knew his daddy, too. There was one worthless railroader for you. He called himself a brakeman. Huh!"

"Is this the same Stan Drussell who works at the City Works office?" I asked incredulously.

Mr. Cully cast his line out again. "That's the one. Ain't more than one Stan Drussell in Eden Springs that I know of."

The earth abides forever, and we are taken up eventually, and the rains fall, and in all things there is a circle, just as in the making of all things there is a unity. I sat in the gently rocking canoe, listening to the wheezing breath of the old man, and thought about how he and Tag had both experienced war and how it had affected them emotionally, and the coincidences of life and the sometimes tragic outcomes of those coincidences. Where had I been? I wondered. What kind of newspaper reporter was I?

Stan Drussell was in a militia unit. I should have known the motive I unconsciously sought was there. I was not imagining things, as my editor had implied, for one form of subterfuge leads to another.

"This is going to get very complicated," I muttered to myself.

"Cast out a little farther, Donny," Mr. Cully said. "You're gonna get caught up in those fallen branches."

As soon as I got home that morning, I began to make phone calls. Mr. Cully had given me the names of two other men in the militia unit: Carson and Milbradt. I decided not to contact Drussell first, but started with Carson. He wasn't home, so I dialed Milbradt. I introduced myself as a reporter for the Banner and told him we wanted to do a story on his group. Milbradt demanded to know how I had gotten his name. When I mentioned Stan Drussell, he relaxed a little.

"Stan told you to call me?" Milbradt asked.

I tried to avoid a direct lie. "I think it's best to talk to the men in the ranks," I said. "For background information, you know."

I must have said something wrong here, because Milbradt's voice became suspicious again. Maybe he wasn't in the ranks.

"Stan told you to call me?" he asked again, this time more belligerently.

"How would I have gotten your name otherwise?" I asked.

There was a long pause, and I realized that Milbradt was thinking about this question.

"I'd better call Stan," he said after a time. "What's your name again?"

I hung up. I had my confirmation. And of course, by the time I found Drussell's number and dialed, the line was busy.

Seventeen

~

What surprises me now as I look back on those early weeks in September is that I wasn't more touched by Tag's story of the missile attack. I should have been, for it was tragic. But there was something about the incident that bothered me. Perhaps everything Tag had told me was true, and I had no tangible reason to doubt, though something caused me to believe he had altered the truth. There were so many questions, and I was tired of questions and of even remotely trying to understand. I only wanted to believe and to be happy for him and for Sylvie.

Sylvie.

I had just returned to my apartment one afternoon when there was a tap on the door. I hoped it wasn't Anne. We had talked for a long time the night I had unplugged the telephone. I had explained that I needed a few days to reflect on where I was going in life, and needed to do it by myself. Some people draw energy from being around others. I had always preferred to be alone while thinking through a problem.

However, when I opened the door, I was surprised to see that it was Sylvie.

"I rode over on my bike," she said, wiping the perspiration from her eyes with the back of her hand. "It's parked by the lamppost outside the watch shop. Will it be all right?"

"It should be," I said.

Her face was flushed from the heat. It did not seem to come from overhead but to rise from the ground; the trees and lawns and shrubs seemed to emanate heat. The air was heavy with the scent of morning glories and honeysuckle.

"I've got iced tea and cold water," I said. "Would you like something?"

"Tea, please."

Sylvie was wearing the gray Air Force T-shirt I had seen before, a pair of black athletic shorts, and running shoes. I had rarely seen her dressed so casually. She dropped down onto the couch by the window.

"I'm sorry about the other night," I offered, as I handed her the iced tea.

She smiled. "It was a special night. I'm glad you were there."

"Really?"

"Why not?" she asked. "You've always been my favorite cousin."

"Right," I said, but I appreciated the compliment anyway.

Sylvie took a sip of the tea. "I talked to Anne. Is there a problem?"

I wasn't prepared for this question. However, I decided not to be defensive.

"No," I replied. "And yes. I mean, there's really no problem with Anne. I'm just trying to sort things out."

"The young crusader," she said. "The boy with the wisdom of Job. You've always tried to save everyone around you, Donny."

I didn't like where this conversation was going. "I can't help it," I said.

"But you've stopped seeing Anne."

"Just temporarily."

Sylvie sighed. "I can only imagine how I would feel if Tag wanted to stop seeing me," she said, then added with a note of disdain, "temporarily."

"Is this why you rode over here? To ask me about Anne?"

Sylvie set down her tea. "Do I need a coaster?"

I almost laughed.

"I thought you might like to walk over to the frozen custard shop and get a cone or something."

"Okay," I said. "Give me a minute to change."

As I was pulling on my shorts in the bedroom, I could hear Sylvie moving around the living room—first to the window and then to the bookcase. The old hardwood floors betrayed her movements. When I came out again, she was holding the Iraqi bayonet.

"Tag gave me that," I explained. "He picked it up in Desert Storm."

"He told me." She pulled the bayonet from the scabbard. "Can you imagine how much it would hurt if . . ." She touched her finger to the point of the bayonet.

"I've thought about that," I said. "It seems dangerous here, but if you were in a war, I imagine it would seem about as dangerous as a toothpick."

She nodded and set the bayonet on the bookshelf beside my copy of Tenny's *New Testament Survey*.

"That's a whole side of Tag I can't relate to," she said with a shudder.

"Has he told you?" I asked.

Sylvie looked at me questioningly. This was something she hadn't expected. She didn't know Tag had told me.

"About Bear?"

"Yes."

She shook her head. "Just horrible. When I think about him trying to . . ."

Sylvie hesitated, and I caught a glimpse of something in her eyes. Was that deception I had just seen, or protectiveness? I could see her wondering. Maybe Tag hadn't told me the whole story.

"Trying to what?" I asked as we went down the stairs and into the bright sunlight. Sylvie's yellow ten-speed was chained securely to the lamppost. We headed up the sidewalk past the general store, the square by the pavilion, and the old movie theater to the frozen custard shop.

"Maybe you should tell me what Tag told you," Sylvie suggested.

"Why?" I asked. "Is there a problem with what he told me?"

I ordered two vanilla cones, and we sat in chairs beneath a green and white striped umbrella on the sidewalk.

"Of course not," she said.

"Listen, Sylvie," I continued. "Something has been nagging me about Tag's story since he told me. I'm sure he left something out."

She licked thoughtfully at her cone. "What did he tell you?"

I watched her face as I talked. Would I be able to tell when the story diverged from the truth? I wondered.

Would there be a glimmer of surprise or hurt? I started at the beginning in Lackland and tried to recite the narrative as best I could. Yet . . . just there, when I mentioned the second Scud; a flicker of confusion in her eyes. So something had been left out or changed. But why? And was it any of my business?

"That's what he told me," I said, finishing the story.

Sylvie touched her forehead with her fingertips and closed her eyes.

"That's not what happened, is it?" I asked tenderly.

She shook her head. "If you only knew." She spoke so softly that I almost couldn't hear. "Poor Tag. Poor, sweet Tag."

"And what about you?" I asked. "Have you told him?"

The tears were coming now, and she set down her cone and wiped her eyes. Sylvie was so sweet, I thought, and so innocent, and why did bad things have to happen to people you loved, and why did life have to be so incredibly, irrevocably difficult? Why couldn't there be a place on this earth where you could be safe and happy if you loved God and tried to lead your life according to His will? Why couldn't there be a place like that? There had been, but Adam had screwed it up and lost paradise. I couldn't really blame him, though, because he didn't realize the enormity of his error. Sometimes that was the price of innocence—not making the right decision through lack of understanding. As I sat and watched Sylvie drying her eyes with a napkin, I told myself I would try to help her, though I did not know what that involved. Perhaps it would come from simply supporting her in any decision she might have to make. And, eventually, I would find out the truth about Tag.

"Let's go," I suggested.

We walked slowly along the brick sidewalk toward the square. I put my arm around her and kissed her on the cheek. To me, she was still my ten-year-old cousin.

"You'll be all right," I said.

"I know I will," she sighed. "We've set a date for December."

"So soon?"

"Tag's afraid they might transfer him after this incident with the jet crash. If that happens, I want to go with him."

"Of course."

I watched as she unlocked the bicycle chain from the lamppost and pushed off.

"See you soon, Donny," she called, as she pedaled up the street.

I waved.

"Give Anne a call!"

"I will," I said truthfully. I would give Anne a call. Sometimes the decisions we make in our lives are not made on a conscious level, but from somewhere down within, and have nothing to do with the way we think. I was not thinking now, only reacting. Jumping into the Trooper, I headed for Genesee Street.

The air felt cool now as I drove out Twenty-ninth Street to Genesee, and I thought that perhaps fall wasn't too far away. I was ready for a change in the temperature—both physically and mentally. My spirits always picked up when the leaves began to turn colors and the air held that hint of a new school year and football games. As I approached the Perrault house, I looked at the second floor to see if the light was on in Anne's room, but it was too early yet. The hard glare of the sun burned orange across the potato field. (Sometimes, after harvesting, we would find small red potatoes in the field, and Anne would fry them with butter and onions and garlic. I had never tasted anything better. To be invited to her house for breakfast was a treat.)

Anne was sitting on the front steps when I opened the gate. A magazine lay at her side. I wondered if Sylvie had called her.

"That didn't take very long," she said. "What happened to all your big problems?"

"I realized I had a bigger one," I answered. "I'm sorry."

She gave me a hug. "Have you eaten? Mom made a pot roast for dinner."

"No."

"Come inside, then."

I took her hand. "Wait a minute."

Anne looked at me.

"You know how I feel about you," I said.

She gazed up at me. "Yes. And you don't have to turn away when you have a problem. I'm here for you."

"I know. It's just that sometimes I get mixed up and need time to let things resolve."

"Couldn't you go for a walk, or fishing, or something?"

"I will from now on."

We kissed, and then she squeezed my hand. "Come on," she urged. "Your place at the table has been set every evening for the past three nights. I don't know how much longer I could have waited."

"It won't happen again," I promised and wondered if she understood the intentions behind my comment.

I followed her through the living room and into the dining room, where I saw a plate and silverware set out for me. It was somehow reassuring to know that I could come back to this, that I hadn't irrevocably damaged my relationship with Anne and her family through my stupidity. I almost felt like crying as I seated myself at the table and gazed at the antique oak sideboard with its blue and white china and green candles. On the far wall was a framed illustration of Jesus looking very serene and intent in brown and white robes, as if someone had just asked him a question: "Lord, will there be a place for me in heaven?" And I thought, Is it possible to find your home away from your family? To feel that a place is more attached to your heart than the home in which you grew up?

I felt that way now.

Anne brought in a steaming platter of roast beef and potatoes and carrots. Then she brought in a gravy boat and a basket of homemade rolls.

I sat there like an idiot with the fork in my hand, biting my lip. Then I muttered a silent prayer and looked at Anne.

"Thank you," I said, but I wasn't referring to the dinner.

She reached across the table and squeezed my hand again affectionately. "We've so much to talk about," she said. "It's horrible not seeing you for so many days."

Eighteen

~

T he weeks seemed to drag on in the crash investigation. I heard from Higdon again, but this
time I refused to talk with him. Tag had been
called in to the JAG office for a third interview, and I
hoped it wasn't due to anything I had said. I had tried to
be honest with Higdon that evening at Darby's, thinking
the truth could only help my friend. But sometimes now I
wondered. Higdon assured me the investigation was
going well and the guilty man would be discovered. I
asked if "guilty" was the appropriate word. If a man was
doing his best and inadvertently made a mistake, did that
make him *guilty*?

"We are trying to place the blame, Mr. Foster, so that
this will not happen again," Higdon explained calmly. "If
a relative of yours was involved in a crash, wouldn't you
want to know why?"

Yes, I would, I told myself. But I wasn't going to con-
cede anything to this man—even though at heart I liked
him.

"Do you have anything for the record?" I asked.

Higdon thought for a moment. "You could print that
we've put off the board results for a few weeks due to a
need for further analysis of the F16 engine."

"Does that mean the crash was not caused by foreign object damage?" I asked.

"The FOD was the definite cause," Higdon replied quickly.

"So what's the problem?"

"This is the Air Force. Sometimes, in an effort to be methodical," he said thoughtfully, "we move slowly."

"Do you know what this is going to do to Roy Dwyer and Richard Taggart?" I asked. "The whole community has turned against them."

"I'm sorry," Higdon said. "But at the moment, it can't be helped."

As I hung up the phone, I felt incredibly sad for Tag. This wasn't fair. He had put up a good front now for two months, thinking that it would soon be over, believing that he could outlast the public pressure. And yet it was not over. The slow torture of malicious gossip and social ostracism would continue. I began to think of him and Dwyer as insects pinned under a glass bowl, like men in stocks whom everyone in the community could walk past and spit on. The situation was becoming intolerable.

So we continued our journey from summer into fall, propelled by a wind whose destination was not always clear—even to us. And as we moved forward, there was no attempt at complication, for life becomes complicated enough by itself. More than complicated; it becomes a maze through which we are obliged to find our own way by use of discernment and conviction. I had never considered my life uncomplicated—what fool could claim that when there were so many struggles to be dealt with each day? Yet I had no indication that I was slowly moving toward an obstruction for which there was no bypass. It began with that first telephone call I received from Tag upon his return to Eden Springs. I had been working on the Cottonwood expansion project story. And then, slowly, ever so subtly, life began to complicate itself. Looking back on it later, I could only shake my head in amazement. When do we suddenly become aware that the tender vines at our feet have grown strong enough to choke us? Is this how conviction enters—as a safeguard to distance us from that possibility?

One morning I awoke and the sky was overcast and swollen gray with rain clouds. The summer was finally over. The rains had begun. I was surprised at how quickly the temperature had dropped. People on the streets were suddenly wearing sweaters and carrying umbrellas. The earth had finally revolved around the sun enough for the autumn to truly begin. And I was happy. As much as I enjoyed the warmth of summer, I appreciated the fall even more. This was my time of the year, my best season for productivity. I felt invigorated by the cool mornings and crisp afternoons. I felt that life had begun again, as if God had energized me with rebirth in the midst of decay.

After lunch at Hazel's, I began to sit in the square for a few minutes each afternoon and breathe in the fresh air before returning to the office. It seemed to help clear my head from the oppressive heat and humidity of summer. I realized there were only a few problems in my life with which I really needed to deal.

While I sat in the square and made my futile plans, life was convoluting itself again, turning and twisting like an injured snake. I should have seen it coming, but I was too focused on my relationship with Anne, and too worried about Tag and Sylvie. I should have expected it, though. My investigation of Drussell and his connection with the militia unit had continued. I had confronted evil, and I should have expected evil to retaliate.

I've tried to retrace the events of that day: where I was beforehand, what I was thinking, if I had inadvertently noticed anything out of the ordinary. But I didn't. I had taken a pizza over to Anne's house that evening, and we had watched a football game on television. It was about ten o'clock when I walked out to my Trooper, tired and stretching in the cool evening breeze. The moon was down, and it was a black night. The light from Anne's porch reflected off the sweet maple trees in her yard, beyond which lay the invisible potato field. It reminded me of that emptiness one feels when gazing at the ocean at night, as if one is standing on the very edge of infinity, or trying to reach up and touch the distant stars. Anne waved goodbye to me from the porch, shivered in the night air, and went inside. I climbed into the Trooper and turned the ignition, but the engine would not start. That was strange, I told myself. It sounded as if the battery was dead.

Opening the hood, I looked inside with my flashlight. The battery cables had been disconnected. That could only mean . . .

A blow struck me painfully on the back of the head, and hands grabbed at me. I was slammed up against the side of the Trooper. I tried to swing my right arm free and strike out, but I was held too firmly.

"Anne!" I cried as a hand covered my mouth. I felt myself being dragged across the road toward the field. How many were there? I wondered. At least three. And why were they dragging me into the darkness of the field? Panicked, I began to kick and struggle, but another blow landed across my neck. Then I hung limp among the hands that pulled and tugged at me. At last I felt the rough, damp earth of the field against my face and was lying with someone's knee pressing into my back.

"We ought to kill you," a voice whispered harshly.

I blinked the dirt out of my eyes and tried to speak, but the breath was knocked out of me.

"Do you hear?"

I nodded.

"And we will, too, if you don't lay off."

Something crashed against my ribs, and I felt a jarring pain. "Maybe you aren't so worried about yourself, Mr. Foster, but you got family and friends. We know all about you."

The knee on my back pressed harder into my shoulder blades.

"Do you understand?" the voice asked.

I nodded again.

"I thought you would. Now we're . . ."

A sudden explosion startled me and caused the man on my back to jerk up.

A shotgun had been fired from the edge of the road.

"Get away from him!" someone shouted.

It was George Perrault, Anne's father.

"Go on, now!" Mr. Perrault demanded again. "I mean it!"

The knee lifted off my back, and I took a deep breath and coughed.

"Easy now, old man," a voice above me said.

"The police are on their way," Mr. Perrault warned.

I heard footsteps running off into the darkness and felt someone bending over me.

"Donny?" Anne asked. "Are you all right?"

"Just let me lie here for a moment."

"Don't try to move," she said, and I felt her hand moving tenderly over my back.

"Does it feel like anything is broken?"

"I don't know."

"Praise God you're alive," she said and began to cry.

"Yes." For a minute there, I had been worried. As I was being dragged across the road, it had all seemed so improbable. My emotions had come in a rush. First I had felt anger, then remorse, and finally contrition. If that had been the end, I asked myself, would I have been ready? I had to think about that for a moment.

Nineteen

~

The police took down my statement, and my editor drove out to see me.

"Well," Thomas said gruffly, as I gazed up at him from the Perrault's couch. "It must have been that antique shop fire. I told you to lay off the hard stuff. You know how those ladies are when they get riled up."

"Right," I muttered through a sore lip.

"I'm putting Charley Oliver on the story. You can brief him in the morning on what's been happening."

"That' s not necessary," I said. "I can handle it."

"You don't understand," Thomas snapped. "You're not some free agent out there reporting for yourself. You're part of the team. If you get taken out, we hand the ball off to someone else. See, the important thing is the team—not the individual player."

I hated it when Ed Thomas pulled out all his old football clichés. But I understood what he meant.

"Okay," I said reluctantly.

"After all," Thomas added, "this isn't an attack against you. It's an attack against the truth. It doesn't matter if you're on the story or not. The Banner still goes on reporting."

"Be careful," I urged.

Anne had insisted that I stay at her house for a few days, and I hadn't argued. When my editor left, I felt very tired and closed my eyes. Some time later, I felt someone spreading a blanket over me and then the light went off. A hand touched my forehead, and Anne's voice spoke softly in my ear: "I'm praying for you."

I fell asleep and dreamed something evil was creeping up on me, like an invisible vapor, and surrounding me. In the dream I jumped up and moved frantically from side to side, but I could not escape. Then I was afraid. The fear came from not being able to see what was moving toward me. I could sense its presence—as if it were more than a vapor—but I couldn't see it. So I stood terrified with my eyes closed. Then, slowly, I became angry and began to shout, "You have no authority over me! I don't belong to you! Get out of here! Go away!"

Then I was awake, and, opening my eyes, I saw Tag smiling down at me.

"Donny," he said. "Settle down. I think you were having a bad dream."

"I was," I muttered and squinted around the room. It was morning. Sunlight was coming in through the living room windows.

"There's a nasty rumor going around that you got into a fight with the waitress at Hazel's. Didn't tip her enough, eh?"

"Listen," I said, pulling myself into a sitting position. "I almost got my backside knocked off last night. So skip the jokes, okay?"

"Sure, Donny," Tag said. "I'm just glad to see someone else taking the hits for a while. I was beginning to think they were all saved for me."

"What are you doing here?" I asked.

Tag suddenly looked hurt. "I wanted to see if you needed anything."

"I need a few things from my apartment, but I can get them myself," I said, trying to stand up and then sitting down quickly.

"Take it easy," Tag said. "Just give me your key and I'll run over to your place right now."

"Where's Anne?"

Tag motioned toward the front door. "She's outside, looking at your Trooper."

"Is it okay?" I asked, concerned.

Tag shrugged. "The window on the driver's side is cracked. How did that happen?"

"With my head, I think."

"Brother. Those guys meant business."

I rubbed my lip. "I guess so."

"Do you know who they were?"

A distant memory of the harsh voice came back to me. I had already mentioned this to the sheriff. "I'm not positive, but it sounded like Joe Milbradt. I only talked to him once on the phone."

"Who's he?" Tag asked.

"A friend of Drussell's."

"But you aren't positive?"

"No."

"That's not much."

"Does it matter?"

"I guess not," Tag said and shrugged. "If you aren't worried."

"No," I said, thinking of the vapor that had crept up silently around me in the dream. "I'm not worried."

"About anything?"

"No."

"Not even me and Sylvie getting married?"

So that was still bothering him. How long would it take for me to regain his confidence?

"Especially not that," I said truthfully. "Now, can I get some rest?"

"Sure," Tag said. "I'll drop by later with your stuff."

"Thanks."

The sheriff found Joe Milbradt at home following the assault on me. When Milbradt came to the door, he was wearing pajamas and looked as if he had been asleep. Milbradt swore that he had gone bowling earlier in the evening and that he had several witnesses to prove it.

One of these was Carson—the other name Mr. Cully had given me. I knew the fix I was in, but I had no way of proving they were lying. I hadn't been able to see their faces, and had only heard Milbradt's voice once on the phone. So my friends in the sheriff's office had suggested that I forget it and keep my eyes open. I had briefed Charley Oliver on the story and he was writing a follow-up article. Word would soon get out that I was off the story. My professional intellect told me not to take it personally. They hadn't come after me because I was Donny Foster, Eden Springs resident, but because I was a Banner reporter. It wasn't personal. But it felt personal. Each time I touched my lip, or felt the ache in my back and neck, it felt personal.

I stayed at Anne's house for two days. When I finally returned to my apartment, pushing the door open wide and hesitating a moment before entering, I felt as if I had been away for a month. And I knew also, as I tossed my bag on the bed and dropped onto the

cushion in the bay window, that my life had begun
that curious alteration of which we are only sometimes
aware. My life in Eden Springs was changing, and I was
left guessing as to where the changes would lead.

Twenty

~

The Dwyer family attended the first church service on Sunday, as usual. This time, however, they arrived late and sat in a back pew. I happened to glance over my shoulder as they entered. The congregation was singing:

> *Be still, my soul: the Lord is on your side.*
> *Bear patiently the cross of grief or pain.*
> *Leave to your God to order and provide.*
> *In every change, He faithful will remain.*

Roy Dwyer's wife sat beside him, and his two little girls—who had inherited their father's fair complexion and reddish hair—sat beside her. Mrs. Dwyer looked as if she was about to cry, and the girls looked frightened. To my dismay and shame, several families who had been sitting near them got up and moved. I tried to attract the attention of our pastor, but he was seated in the first row, waiting for the worship music to end before he moved up to the platform. Giving Anne's hand a squeeze, I motioned for her to follow me. We got up quietly and moved to the back row. I sat down next to Dwyer and nodded to him in greeting. He looked angry and humiliated. His jaw was clenched, and he held tightly to his wife's hand. So this is what happens when they come to us for solace, I told myself. They come for acceptance and we give them humiliation. They come for mercy and we give them rejection.

And who was I to talk? I had been overcome with self-pity because I had been slammed up against a car. At least I hadn't been required to go through this. The community hadn't turned against me. That was a lot worse. No matter who was to blame in the crash report, we would never be able to make it up to the Dwyers now. We had let them down when they needed us most. And what did that say about us? Where did that put our hearts?

Roy Dwyer fumbled with the hymnal for a moment and then slammed it back into the holder with frustration. He put his hands up to his face and then leaned back and breathed hard. I was just about to ask if he was all right when he pushed past me and stood up in the aisle. He motioned for his family to follow, and they slipped quickly from the pew and headed toward the door. I was worried now because I had seen the look in Dwyer's eyes—a kind of controlled hysteria. I was suddenly nervous for him. When does a man decide that he has had enough? I wondered. Did he see a look of doubt in his daughters' eyes each time they gazed at him? In his wife's eyes? And how long could he live with that? What did it do to his insides, if he cared about his family's respect? And what about his position in the Air Force? Would it ever be the same?

After the service we walked out to the steps, and I couldn't help thinking about Tag sitting there so many years ago, praying through the night that his father would survive leukemia. I could only shake my head in disbelief.

He was one of my closest friends, and yet there was evidently so much I didn't know about him. It made me wonder if we could ever really know anyone. But of course, so many of us didn't know ourselves—how could we expect to know each other?

A black pickup truck was parked across the street.

"Who's that?" Anne asked.

"Beats me," I said, still thinking about Tag.

"Well, he's looking straight at you," she said. "He must be someone you know."

I shaded my eyes and looked across the street. It was Clifton Howard. When he saw me looking at him, he motioned for me to come over to his truck.

"I'll just be a second," I said to Anne.

"Is this anything I should be worried about?" she asked.

"No, no. Cliff's okay."

"Then I'll be inside," Anne offered. "I have some questions to ask about the luncheon next week."

I crossed the street to the truck.

Howard reached a hand through the open window.

"Hey, Foster," he said. "I heard you got into some trouble."

"A bit," I said, surprised. The manager of Kaplan Construction was a long way from my circle of friends. "Who told you?"

Howard shrugged and wiped a hand across his mustache. "Word gets around."

"I guess so."

"So you're okay?"

"I'm fine."

He gripped the steering wheel. "I also heard you're not on the bid story anymore."

"They gave it to another reporter."

"The militia story?"

"Same."

"That's okay, isn't it?"

"I guess so."

Howard glanced at his watch. "Well, I'd better shove off. I'm on my way out to Wingert Lake. Gonna do a little fishing."

"I've done that myself."

I noticed a rifle perched in the rack behind his head. It was a semiautomatic with a four-round magazine.

"Though I usually use a rod and bait, myself," I said, smiling.

Howard turned and looked at the rifle. "Oh, yeah. I forgot it was back there."

"What part of the lake do you fish?" I asked.

"Along the east bank," he said, starting his truck. "Well, I need to get going. Take care of yourself, Foster."

"I'll try," I said and waved as he drove slowly up the street.

Anne was waiting for me on the church steps. I told her what Cliff had said.

"He's the man who complained about you investigating the bid story, isn't he?" she asked. "The one who questioned your integrity?"

"It's funny," I replied. "I haven't seen him for months, and now he waits outside the church to see how I'm doing."

"That sounds really nice to me," Anne said thoughtfully. "Maybe he's sorry for what he said before."

"I suppose so."

She took my arm. "So where are we going for lunch?"

I gazed at the brilliant leaves of a red oak tree on the lawn. "Let's drive out to the old cider mill. They have great food, and we haven't been there for a long time."

"That sounds like fun," Anne said. "And on the way, we'll talk."

"About what?" I asked.

"About . . . things," she said. "Life. God. You know."

I didn't know exactly, but I was willing.

"Okay," I said. "But that's going to take at least one good squeeze before we get into the car."

Anne smiled and slipped her arms around my waist. She smelled like autumn, and bonfires at night, and snuggling beside each other on the couch, and perfume, and promises fulfilled.

"How was that?" she asked.

"Great," I said. "For the moment."

"Let's go," she pleaded. "I'm hungry."

So we headed out Route J into the colorful splashes of oak woods, and rolling pastures, and fields.

For the next several weeks, Tag and Sylvie were busy with their wedding plans. The date had been set for the second Saturday in December, and Sylvie had signed up for wedding gifts at Nelligan's on the square. There was no point in my going to Nelligan's without Anne. I didn't know a fork from a spoon when it came to that kind of thing. But I could throw Tag a party. I was good at that, so I started making plans. My concern was that no one would come. But maybe the crash investigation would be over by then and Tag would be vindicated. I certainly hoped so, for everyone's benefit.

It was getting more and more difficult to see Tag. He was still good-natured when we were together, but he had withdrawn completely from life in Eden Springs. He had been rejected by his friends in the Air Force and the community. So he kept to himself—like a man desperately holding his breath underwater, hoping someone will come along and save him before he sinks completely. Yet Tag was not bitter. I began to think bitterness stemmed from a belief that we deserved special consideration above and beyond what we received. And if that were true, then the opposite of bitterness was humility. I had never thought of Tag as humble; he had always possessed a solid confidence in himself and his abilities. But perhaps he had learned things in Saudi Arabia which had given him a new perspective.

This reminded me of my uncle Walter.

Uncle Walter was my father's eldest brother. As a boy he had suffered from an undefined illness and had been, at my grandmother s request, removed from school. While the other boys in the family had played baseball in the sandlot behind the house, Uncle Walter was forced to sit on the back steps and watch. He was slow, everyone said. This was true in some ways, and you particularly noticed it in his slow and carefully articulated speech. But he could tell you the batting average of any baseball player since Babe Ruth. He listened avidly to major league games on an old radio in his room. I could remember Uncle Walter sitting beside his radio, leaning forward expectantly, his eyes focused far away, a shy smile spreading across his face under his large nose whenever a good play was made or his team scored a run. I could still remember the soft yellow glow of his desk light beside the radio, and the creak of his wooden chair as he would turn and look at me, amused.

I never told anyone how much I loved Uncle Walter, or that I secretly admired and identified with him. I loved him because Uncle Walter was flawed, and I have always loved people more, my heart has gone out to them more, when they are flawed. Among other things, at the age of nine, I had envied the fact that Uncle Walter still lived at home even though he was fifty. How wonderful it would be, I imagined then, to always remain at home, to never be forced to leave your parents, to always reside in the warm, loving protection of your family. (That was to change soon, but I did not know it then.) Not until I became an adult did I realize the folly of such a life. Uncle Walter had been trapped behind the four walls of that house near the sandlot. He had never been given the chance to see how far he could go. Other men could have become bitter about this, but if Uncle Walter had been bitter, he had hidden it well.

The question I asked myself, when I felt confused about life and the way things were turning out, was about outcomes. Did Uncle Walter fail in life because he was never given the chance to really live? Or was his life full and meaningful because he had accepted his fate and lived each day with a sense of servitude and affection? I knew what my pastor would tell me. He would explain that the only important life was the life we lived through God, and only God could judge a life's value. But it was something I thought about. I viewed Uncle Walter's lack of bitterness as a form of wisdom, and I thought about this when I observed Tag's reaction. Perhaps the inherent acceptance of responsibility was the understanding of the consequences. If you accepted the responsibility, then you could not be bitter about the outcome. Not unless an unfair amount of pressure was involved. Then you were not bitter about the consequences, but about the way you were treated by people.

Twenty-One

As the last days of October seemed to drift away with the leaves, my work at the Banner continued. Reporting for a newspaper is like working at the edge of an inky black pit into which you toss your time and energy (much like Tony Hamilton's statement about owning a boat). When I first began my job as a reporter, it sometimes amazed me that stories I had worked on under pressure of deadline—working right up to the last minute, receiving the important telephone call fifteen minutes before the story went to the editor—ended up as garbage wrappers the next afternoon. But there were perks also. One of these came in knowing what was happening in the community, being kept informed of the inside gossip of politics and society. So in some ways I was not surprised when the telephone rang and it was Higdon. Perhaps he felt bad about asking me to inform on a friend, or perhaps he had experience with the media. In any event, this time he had called to provide me with information.

"I thought you'd like to know the board has reached a decision," he explained. "An official statement will be released tomorrow morning."

"Really?" I asked. "Who was it?"

Higdon paused, and I suddenly realized how difficult this decision was going to be. Both Tag and Dwyer were good men. However, one was going to walk away, and the other would have his career ruined. How could I wish that on anyone? I almost didn't want Higdon to tell me. Why had he called, anyway? I wondered. To break the news, because it was Tag?

The JAG officer sounded as if he were reading a prepared statement. "The board has found Tech Sergeant Roy Dwyer at fault in the crash of the F16 on 17 July," Higdon said. "Previous to take-off, Tech Sergeant Dwyer assisted with a periodic inspection of the F16 engine. At that time, while helping on an engine borescope, Tech Sergeant Dwyer left a rag under the engine cowling."

"What a shame," I said.

"A court-martial will be held next July to determine the consequences of the findings."

"How is he supposed to live until then?" I asked.

"It's terrible, I know," Higdon said. "But that's the procedure."

"Have Taggart and Dwyer been informed?"

"Yes."

"Then I'd better go," I said. "Thanks for calling."

I hit the disconnect button and dialed Tag's number. The line was busy, so I called Sylvie.

Melissa answered.

"Have you heard?" I asked.

"Yes," she said, her voice trembling. "Tag called a few minutes ago. Sylvie went over there."

"I'm really sorry about Dwyer," I said. "But I'm glad it wasn't Tag."

"Me too," Melissa sighed.

The night air was cold as I sped over to Tag's house, and I rolled up my side window, which had just been replaced. Except for a small cut above my left eye where my forehead had smacked the glass, all traces of the potato field incident had been erased. Now it was time for celebration. I couldn't wait to see the expression on Tag's face. He must be so excited! Everything was different now. The ostracism was over. His life in the Air Force would continue as before.

The wind blew leaves across the street in front of my headlights as I turned onto Gardner. As I approached the Taggart home, a sudden thought struck me. What was I doing? Sylvie had just gone over to be with Tag. What was the point in my being present? I had already intruded on the marriage proposal. Was I now going to barge in on this moment of happiness? Slowing the Trooper to a halt about a half-block from the house, I gazed through the dark shrubs and saw the porch lights twinkling. If I had just been given a reprieve, I asked myself, how would I react? Would I want to throw a party or would I want to spend a few quiet moments alone with my fiancée? I knew the answer to that question. I wasn't Tag, of course, but I knew the answer.

Passing the house, I dimmed my headlights and kept rolling. Sylvie's car was parked at the curb. I could see them through the large front window, holding each other as if they were dancing, but there was no music that I could hear. This was the true celebration, I told myself— the music of silent, tender joy.

Anne was working the three-to-eleven shift, so I drove over to the hospital. When I entered the intensive care unit, she was going over a chart with an aide. She smiled happily when she saw me.

"I just got a call from Captain Higdon," I whispered, taking her aside. "Dwyer left the rag in the engine. It wasn't Tag."

"Oh, my," she said. "I'm so happy for him."

Then I shook my head sadly. "I feel sorry for the Dwyers."

"We should go over there tomorrow and see if they need anything."

"If they let us in."

"Maybe they won't," Anne said. "But we should try."

I glanced at my watch. It was half past eight. Anne didn't get off work for another two and a half hours.

"How about a cup of coffee when you finish?" I asked.

She glanced at her chart. "I may have to work late. How about lunch tomorrow?"

I recited the weekly menu in my head. Wednesday was pork chops.

"Sure. About a quarter to twelve?"

"Okay."

I gave her a hug.

"You know," she said, "the last time you were in here, the aides thought you were a doctor."

"I could be," I boasted, and then added, "except for the blood."

"They key is not to associate blood with pain," Anne offered.

"I'll stick to ink. I love the smell of a fresh newspaper in the morning."

"You're a little weird sometimes," she said and laughed.

"Sorry."

"Don't be. I like it when you're a little weird."

Someone called to Anne from the nurse's station.

"I need to go," Anne said. "We're expecting one of our patients to pass on tonight."

"It must be rough."

"She's saved. That makes it easier."

"Yes."

Anne started toward the nurse's station and then stopped. "If you see Tag, tell him how happy I am for him."

"He's with Sylvie," I said.

"I thought he would be."

Twenty-Two

I waited until the following morning to call Tag. When he answered, the burden of stress seemed to have lifted from his voice. He sounded younger, more enthusiastic.

"Congratulations," I said. "It's over."

"Yes," he sighed. "For me, anyway."

"So let's celebrate. How about breakfast? Nothing better than fried eggs and hash browns at Hazel's on a fall morning."

"Sure," he said. "Come on over."

I pulled on a pair of jeans and a flannel shirt and made it over to Tag's house in twenty minutes. I could hear the telephone ringing as I came up the steps.

"Hey, Donny," Tag said, opening the screen. "Come on in. I have to get the phone."

"Where's your mom?"

"She's having breakfast with some of her friends. I guess she feels like going out now."

I could imagine.

Tag picked up the phone, and his face grew tense.

"Is something wrong?" I asked.

Tag nodded.

"When did she call?" he asked into the receiver.

And then:

"You're sure he's not just out someplace to be by himself?"

He listened.

"Where are they meeting?"

He made a note on a piece of paper.

"I'll be there," he said and then, glancing at me, added, "Is it okay if I bring a buddy? He knows the area."

Tag nodded and then said, "Hold on."

He looked at me. "Dwyer disappeared sometime in the night. His wife's afraid he might do something stupid. And if he doesn't show up for the 10:30 board hearing, he'll be AWOL. Can you help us find him?"

"Sure," I said.

"She thinks he may have gone out to a deer stand by the river. Some of the guys from the squadron are meeting out there."

"I'll be glad to help."

"Good."

Tag spoke into the receiver again. "Tell them we're on our way."

Breakfast at Hazel's was out now, so we quickly made two ham sandwiches and hurried out to the Trooper.

The fastest way to the bluff from Gardner Avenue was to drive through the downtown area and then head west. I slowed for a traffic light swaying in the wind above the intersection of First and Main, and then turned onto Levee Road. Gazing through the trees, I could see the river flowing narrow and muddy. It had rained during the night, and the ground was wet with sodden leaves and weeds. The trees along the bank were stained dark with moisture. The air was cold and smelled of wood smoke and rain. I glanced at my tennis shoes. If we were going to be tramping around through the woods, it would have been better if I had worn my duck boots.

A group of cars and trucks were gathered at the edge of the woods by the bluff. At least twenty men were huddled together and talking. One of them was looking at a map.

"Morning, Lieutenant," Tag said as we walked up to them.

"Morning, Taggart," the officer said. "Who's this?"

"A friend of mine. Donny knows these woods pretty well."

"Good," the officer said. "Dwyer's wife thinks he went to a deer stand somewhere down there by the river. Does anyone know where that could be?"

We all shook our heads.

"Then we'll have to spread out. About fifty paces between each man. Ready?"

We formed a long line and began to walk west with the river on our right. Gazing at the woods ahead of us, I thought of the tangled undergrowth and narrow ravines with steep, muddy sides. Deer stands were usually built on high ground, or at the edge of the woods. I didn't know of any that were built in dense brush.

"Let's stay close to the river," I said to Tag. "It gets too hilly back in there to see anything."

"I think you're right," Tag said.

We moved forward through the trees.

After fifteen minutes, we stopped and called down the line to make sure no one had gotten lost. I could hear the men's voices as they thinned out in the distance. Everyone was accounted for. Then we continued on, shifting a little bit north as the river turned.

It was odd, but as we trod through the clinging brush and low branches, a memory came back to me of Grandfather Graham's old hunting rifle. He had kept it in his closet, set deep in a corner and hidden behind a faded robe. I was not allowed to take out the rifle except by permission. On those occasions when I was allowed, I would open the door and be struck by the smell of mothballs and old flannel shirts, trousers worn shiny on the creases from ironing, and leather shoes polished to the softness of an old harness. The rifle was small with a heavy barrel and a worn stock, but to me (as a boy) it was an artifact from the Civil War, of Davy Crockett, of the Colonial Militia and its fight against the Indians, of a lone frontier scout slipping silently through the deep forests of the past, in search of the ever-mysterious land beyond. All those thoughts had come to me when I ran my fingers over the smooth stock—and all those things were me. I was that frontier scout, I had walked sentry duty through the snow at Valley Forge, and I had paddled upriver with Lewis and Clark.

When I asked Grandpa Graham if I could shoot the rifle, he had touched his hand to the barrel thoughtfully and said no, that the old gun no longer worked. The last time he had tried to fire it—many years ago—the hammer had broken off and blown back past his ear. He only kept it around now for the memories. I wondered what memories he had of the gun, and if they were like mine, but we never talked about it. He would only sit there with me on his bed and look at the rifle for a few minutes and then, gazing off distantly, say it was time to put the old gun away. I would set it awkwardly back in the corner—for it was heavy—cover it over again with the faded robe, and then close the door. Then I would go outside and pick up a stick or piece of wood and run through the forests of my imagination—even though I was only in the backyard of a small Midwestern town.

I often wondered what had happened to the rifle. Once when I was a teenager, I had broken the rules and opened the closet door without asking, but the rifle was not there. When I inquired about it later, my mother told me that the rifle had been given to my grandfather by his father. I knew that my grandfather's parents had died when he was nine years old, and he had been sent to live in a series of foster homes. My grandfather had had a difficult childhood. Yet the rifle had always stayed with him. I wondered if, instead of Colonial forests and Indians, my grandfather's imagination had taken him back to an earlier time, when he was a boy and had spent time with his father. Those would have been precious memories for him, and I could better understand now that distant gaze that came into his eyes as we sat together on the bed. Naturally he would have wanted to put the rifle away after a few minutes, for memories cannot be shared—even by a boy who gazed at his tennis shoes and saw moccasins.

I walked along now in silence, thinking about Tag's experiences in the war, and of Mr. Cully on Iwo Jima. The leaves crackled under my feet, and I thought about the old rifle and how so many of our most precious childhood memories are made up of little inconsequential moments. So what made them stick? I wondered. What did they represent that made them so important?

Above my head, sunlight streamed through the dappled leaves. I thought about Anne and wondered how late she had worked. Then I thought about the Cottonwood bid proposals, Stan Drussell, and Clifton Howard. There was something missing, but I was off the story now. In time, everything would sort itself out. Someday there would be an answer.

A fox bolted from its hiding place and raced through the trees in front of me. I stopped to catch my breath and to wipe my face. I had managed to work up a sweat, even though the air was cool in the woods.

Tag called softly at my side, "Donny."

He pointed off to the right, and I looked up and saw something brown and square in the trees. It was built on long poles about twenty feet off the ground.

"That's it," he said. "Let's get closer."

We moved quietly toward the stand.

Twenty-Three

It seemed overly dramatic for us to be sneaking up on the little shelter. After all, Roy Dwyer was a good man with a wife and family. But I had seen that look in his eyes at church, and I was worried that he might take a shot at us if we got too close. I didn't know if Dwyer had a gun, but it was better not to take a chance. Tag apparently felt the same way, because he motioned for us to take cover behind a thick spruce tree.

"Can you see the ladder?" he asked.

I looked around the far side of the trunk. "Yeah, it's on the back side."

"Keep an eye on it."

"What are you going to do?"

"If he's up there, I'll try to talk him down."

Tag stepped out into the clearing.

"Roy!" he called. "It's Taggart. Are you up there?"

I heard a definite creak in the floor of the deer stand and tensed.

"Stay away!" shouted a voice. It was Roy Dwyer, and he sounded strained and exhausted.

"Listen, Roy," Tag said. "It's okay. You can come down. Everything will be all right."

"I'm not a criminal!" Dwyer shouted.

"We know that," Tag said. "Come on down."

I heard another creak at the back of the stand, and then a figure slid quickly down the ladder and hit the ground. It was Dwyer. He scrambled to his feet and took off in the direction of the river.

"Come back, Roy!" Tag shouted and began to run.

I called to the other men and started after them.

I had been a runner in school and could move fast, but Dwyer was ripping through the woods at a frantic pace. I caught up with Tag as we reached a bluff over-looking the river. It was a long way down.

"Where is he?" I asked, breathing hard.

"Down there," Tag gasped and pointed.

I could see Dwyer half scrambling, half falling down the slope. He was almost at the bottom. From there the bank was clear in either direction.

"There has to be a better way," I suggested.

"He'll go upstream," Tag said. "The other direction would take him back to Eden Springs. We can follow him from up here until we find a place to go down."

Dwyer reached the bottom of the bluff and stood for a moment, looking up and down the river. He seemed con-fused, and I felt tremendously sorry for him.

"Dwyer!" I called. "Roy!"

He looked up at us and then began to run again.

"Let's go," Tag said.

We raced along the top of the bluff for half a mile before the ground began to slope toward the river. Finally we reached a ravine that cut straight down to the water. We scrambled down, slipping on wet leaves and mud, and then began to jog upstream. I was getting tired, but Tag seemed to be driven by an undefined force. He pushed ahead, a determined look on his face. I imagined there was more to this incident for him than just catching Dwyer. Perhaps it wasn't even Dwyer that he was after, but Bear. Whose face did he see on the running man ahead of us? I wondered. Was he trying to change outcomes? Was he trying to make up for something he had lost?

Far upstream I could see the trellis bridge. Glancing at my watch, I saw that it was half past ten. The local from Kansas City would be coming through soon. I wondered if Roy Dwyer knew about the train.

Time and distance take on a varied perspective when you are in a chase. We had already covered at least a mile since we had spotted the deer stand, but it didn't seem half as far as the tedious walk we had made from the cars. I could see where Dwyer was headed. A trail led from the river along a bank to the bridge.

"Roy!" Tag shouted. "Stop!"

"I'm not a criminal!" Dwyer shouted back and began to climb the bank.

"This isn't the way!" Tag shouted. "Please, Roy!"

Just then I heard the distant sound of the local. It was about a half-mile away.

Dwyer reached the bridge and began to cross. A narrow wooden plank lay on either side of the tracks, wide enough for a man to walk without falling through the open ties. It would have been a hazardous crossing on the best of days, but now there was a train approaching from the other direction. I could hear the blaring horn of the local as it neared the bridge.

Tech Sergeant Dwyer was caught. If he turned back now, we had him. Other members of the squadron were coming up the bank.

Tag said, "He's gonna get himself killed."

"What can we do?" I asked. "The train is coming. We can't go out there."

"I can't . . ." Tag muttered. "Not another . . ." He stepped out onto the narrow footboards.

"Wait a minute!" I called. "He'll come back!"

"I don't think so!" Tag shouted.

Dwyer saw the train coming and then looked at us. He hesitated for a moment, and I wondered if he was thinking about surrendering. Then he seemed to make up his mind and moved over to the railing.

It was at least a hundred feet down to the water. With the heavy rains, the current was flowing in a muddy rush against the pilings.

My heart sank. Oh, no, I thought.

"Roy!" Tag shouted. "You don't have to do this. It's not over yet!"

The train was coming on fast now, blowing its horn. I could see the engine through the trees.

"Roy!" Tag shouted.

Dwyer swung a leg over the railing.

"Roy! No!" Tag shouted and began to run.

The next few moments have been etched in my memory forever, and yet the details do not come back with clarity. It is almost as if I had experienced the situation in a dream: Dwyer climbing over the railing and hanging outwards, his hands on the railing and his feet braced against a girder. There was nothing below him except a hundred-foot drop to the surging water. In my mind I saw him releasing his grip and falling backwards, falling, falling; but in reality he continued to hang on. What was he thinking? I wondered. Was he praying? Saying goodbye? Or adding up the odds? What does a man think about when he is dangling from a bridge? And then, amazingly, he pulled himself up and swung his legs back over the railing. The train had reached the bridge now, and I could feel the vibration as the oppressingly heavy, pounding wheels rolled onto the tracks. Tag was on one side of the trellis and Dwyer on the other. The train was rolling toward them, the horn blaring. Tag was shouting, but I couldn't hear what he was saying. I had breathed a sigh of relief when I saw Dwyer slide back over the railing onto the footboards. But then I gasped when I saw him casually, almost unhesitatingly, step in front of the onrushing engine.

I turned away. I had covered the story of a teenager who had been hit by a train a year before, and this was nothing I wanted to remember.

"Lord, help us," I prayed fervently.

Then I heard someone next to me—I think it was the lieutenant—shouting at one of the other men in the squadron.

"Did he get him?! Where are they?! Can you see them?!"

I realized then that something must have happened— something unbelievable. For if Dwyer was truly still alive, and not mangled into something unrecognizable or pitched into the river below, then Tag must have intervened.

Twenty-Four

The few minutes it took for the train to cross the trellis bridge seemed interminable. As it flashed past us, we crouched and gazed through the clattering wheels to see if we could spot them. But the angle was wrong, so we had to wait until the caboose passed and then we began to run. I didn't think about the narrow footboards or my fear of heights as I hurried onto the bridge. They should be there, I told myself. But they weren't, and I began to feel sick. What was I going to tell Sylvie? I asked myself.

Then I saw movement, an arm and leg sticking up near the railing. They were not on the boards but had fallen onto a small maintenance platform that jutted out from the girders like a telephone booth with metal gratings for windows. Tag was lying on his back and shoulders with Dwyer on top of him. Tag was holding on tightly, but I could see that the fight had gone out of Dwyer. His face was ashen, and his body was trembling. The men from the squadron reached down and pulled the tech sergeant up by the arms. He was limp, and they had to support him. Next came Tag. I saw a flash of pain in his eyes as he stood up. He had landed hard on his back and side. He was smiling, but it wasn't from amusement. Did he realize how close he had come? I wondered.

The train slowed to a halt beyond the bridge, and the engineer came running back to us.

"Were they killed?" he asked, flushed. "They just ran in front of me. I've been driving for twelve years, and . . ."

"We have two injured men here," the lieutenant interrupted. "Can you take them into Eden Springs?"

The railroader nodded.

We helped Dwyer and Tag onto the train, and the airmen got on with them. There was no point in my staying aboard. This was an Air Force issue now. The engineer would radio ahead and make sure the SPs were waiting.

I gazed up at the sky. The rain clouds had blown off to the east, and the sun was out again. I glanced at my watch and saw that it was a few minutes after eleven. I had made lunch plans with Anne, but I would never make it now—unless I took the train. It was beginning to roll.

"Why not?" I muttered and jumped onto the loading step. Anne could drive me out to the bluff later. My pants were too muddy to sit in a seat, so I remained on the step. As the train picked up speed, I watched the bridge and the woods fall behind. There was something in my jacket pocket, and I reached in and pulled out a smashed ham sandwich. Breakfast, I thought. It didn't look very appetizing.

By the time we reached the little station at Eden Springs, Tag was feeling better. A blue and white security police car was parked beside the tracks. Two SPs in blue berets were waiting. I watched as Dwyer was escorted down to the platform.

"Are you going on to the base?" I asked Tag.

He stretched his neck and groaned. "No. I need a hot shower and some rest. Want to catch a ride?"

He was referring to the SP car. They were putting Dwyer in now.

"Thanks, but I'll walk."

Tag climbed stiffly into the car.

"By the way," I remarked. "I'm really proud of you. That was amazing—what you did for Dwyer back there."

He shrugged. "You'd have done the same for me, right?"

"Sure," I commented and smiled.

Walking home, crossing the brick streets with people passing on the sidewalks, I wondered if I would have risked my life to save Tag's under similar circumstances. Probably I would have, but there was an assumption that followed that line of thought—that I would have been successful. Actually, I didn't know how Tag had done it. When I had turned away, not wanting to see Dwyer struck by the train, the engine had almost reached him. Somehow Tag had managed, within that split second of time, to throw himself against Dwyer and knock him off the tracks. It was remarkable and foolishly brave. I could only assume that the risk he had taken was to purge himself of the anguish that had begun in the desert and had continued as a lingering wound. I hoped his mind would rest easy now that he had made this effort to save . . . whom? Bear? For it must have been Bear he had seen when he threw himself across those tracks, felt the crushing steel press so close to him, grabbed at the open cage instead of plummeting through the girders. I hoped the effort had brought him some type of resolution, even though he knew Bear was all right. I had already explained that to him, though perhaps my reassurance was not enough. Those nights on the church steps praying for his father had caused him to doubt.

Anne was waiting for me at Hazel's. The cafe was crowded, as usual, but she had managed to find us a table by the window. She looked shocked when she glanced up and saw my appearance. There hadn't been enough time for me to change.

"What have you been doing?" she asked, brushing a leaf off my jacket. "Hunting?"

I slipped into the chair across from her. "Have you ordered yet?" I asked, gulping my water.

Anne shook her head.

"Then let's order first. It's a long story."

The waitress came over. I ordered the daily special, and Anne ordered a bowl of soup. Gazing up at the waitress as she scribbled quickly with her pencil, I subconsciously ran my tongue over my healed lip, thinking about Tag's joke. For some reason I was feeling especially good this morning—despite the events that had taken place at the trellis bridge. And why not? Hadn't everything turned out okay? There was still cause for celebration, wasn't there? And then, from far back in my thoughts, came the memory of the old rifle in the closet. Why was I still thinking about that? I wondered with irritation. I glanced out the window to the brick-front stores and offices of Holden Street and thought of all the times I had walked along that sidewalk with my grandfather. There was the hardware store with its wooden bins of nails and tools hanging from clips on the pegboard walls; the tobacco shop that smelled of warm winter evenings; the ice cream shop where Grandfather had taken me for a cone after we had accomplished our errands; the bookstore with its display of children's books in the corner window. It had never occurred to me that there might come a time when I could no longer walk along that street with my fingers slipped affectionately into my grandfather's hand. Directly across the street was the old Tivoli Theater, where my cousin Philipp and I had waited once after a matinée of *The Sons of Robin Hood*. We had stood there with Turkish taffy breath and wild images of swashbuckling adventurers in our minds until Grandpa Graham had come to pick us up in his white Chevy. It seemed like everyone had a white Chevy then. And now I wished there was someone I could talk to about that rifle. It seemed as if there should still be someone. Always, when anything good happened, I felt as if there should be someone to whom I could say, "Look . . . See what's happened!"

But that time was gone now.

Still, I had the beautiful young woman sitting across from me who was pretending to enjoy her soup because she knew how much I liked this cafe. That was something. She was someone I could turn to and say, "Look!"

We are nurtured by our parents when we come into this world, and protected by our families when we go out, I told myself. And in the middle, we rely on God.

What else could we expect? Nothing more, but wasn't that enough? Wasn't the knowing that all this would one day fade away and that the people we cared about most in this world would be waiting for us in the next enough? Yes. And then we could talk, and I would discover why an old rifle behind a faded robe in a yellowed closet meant so much to me.

Twenty-Five

"Did I ever tell you about my grandfather's old rifle?" I asked Anne.

"I don't think so," she mused. "Is that what you were doing this morning—shooting the rifle?"

"No," I answered, embarrassed. I began to tell her about Tag and Dwyer, the chase through the woods, and the incident on the trellis bridge. Anne's eyes widened as the story progressed. When I had finished, she stared thoughtfully into the distance.

"That's incredible," she said finally, her tone somber. "God bless Tag."

"Yes," I agreed. "I think God has blessed Tag. But I don't think he realizes it."

"Most of us probably don't realize how much we've been blessed," Anne said.

"Maybe," I agreed. "But you couldn't talk about it—even if you knew. It would come across as pride."

Anne nodded. "Maybe with the awareness comes an awesome feeling of responsibility, like 'Whoa, look what God's done for me!' and that would make you feel too humble to say anything."

"It has for me," I said and smiled.

"I'm sure," Anne laughed.

The waitress came with our check.

"Do you think the Air Force will do anything special for Tag?" Anne asked, as we stepped out to the crisp, sunny afternoon. "That was such a brave thing he did."

"I hope so."

"Are you going to write it up for the newspaper?"

"I've been trying to decide. It would be good PR for Tag, but another stone for Dwyer."

"Man Saves Friend by Jumping in Front of Train," Anne said, as if she were reading a headline. "That sounds pretty good to me."

"Yes," I said. "It does. And we don't have many stories like that these days."

"Not enough trains, I guess," Anne said, laughing.

"No," I sighed. "Not enough trains."

So I wrote the story about Tag and Dwyer, and it was accompanied by a photograph of the trellis bridge.

Higdon made the official announcement about Dwyer being found guilty, and I covered it for the Banner. Captain Mark Wayland was slowly recovering at the VA hospital. The investigation was finished. There would be a court-martial in July. Our pastor had driven out to Emerson to talk with Dwyer and offer him a word of encouragement. I wondered what kind of encouragement you can give a man who has stepped in front of a train, but God works in his own ways, and it was not my place to presume.

The weeks passed as I worked at the Banner. In my spare moments, I thought about Tag and the Scud missile attack and the scene on the bridge. It seemed that my friend had already seen too much in this life; had risked too much. Did God set higher obstacles before some of us than before others? I wondered. If the goal was to break a man down until he realized that he was dust, and that nothing existed or could exist without the Almighty, then there would have to be different levels of hardship—just as there were different levels of men. And what was my level? I wondered. Had I already reached bottom, knowing that my only hope for salvation was to cling to the Lord with all my strength? Perhaps, but who would ever know?

Then one night I awakened at half past three in the morning. I had been dreaming that I was standing on the trellis bridge in Dwyer's place, with the train rushing at me. There was no one else on the bridge, and somehow I had pulled out my grandfather's old rifle and had begun to fire at the approaching engine. Even as I was busily slamming back the bolt and the engine was almost on top of me, in my sleep I was thinking: So this is what the rifle means to me—protection. For some distant reason, it has come to represent protection. Then I couldn't hear the engine anymore, and I thought about seeing Clifton Howard's rifle hanging in the back of his truck.

What did a rifle represent for Clifton Howard? I wondered.

I had awakened then, a cold thought racing through my mind. Opening my eyes in the darkness, I began to think. What would I do if my company needed a contract to stay in business? Pray about it? Yes. But if I didn't have faith, would I be desperate enough to try and rig the construction bids? And how would I do that in a way that didn't appear obvious?

Getting out of bed, I walked into the living room and looked out the bay window. The square was silent and lonely. The wind had picked up from the west. Suddenly the idea didn't seem so fantastic, and I began to feel a nervous tension growing in my stomach. Howard could have guessed that the bid from the big-city company would be too high. But not the Braynard submission; a local competitor would have calculated the same construction and labor costs. So Howard had to nullify the Braynard bid somehow. But how? The idea involved a complicated scheme with Stan Drussell at the center. Did Howard know Drussell? If not, how had he gotten Drussell to cooperate? A bribe? $1.8 million was a lot of money.

Walking into the kitchen, I filled a glass with water. $1.8 million—or a percentage of it anyway—would also buy a lot of weapons. A feeling of cold spread through me. It had not been necessary for Howard to bribe Drussell, I told myself, because they were in the same militia unit.

Going to my desk, I pulled out a piece of typing paper and a pencil and began to make a diagram. First I jotted down Howard's name. Then I drew a line from this to Drussell's name. This connection seemed perfectly logical. Then I drew a line from Drussell's name to that of Mary Leighton.

Setting down the pencil and rubbing my eyes, I gazed at the three names. Assuming that Howard and Drussell knew each other, the connections were possible. But what about Mary Leighton? I could have sworn she was telling the truth. And then there was her comment about not wanting to be involved in anything immoral. Was Mary in on this? I asked myself. A member of our church?

Picking up the pen again, I jotted down Mary's name and drew a line to Drussell's. A second line ran from her name to Howard's. It was all beginning to fit too neatly.

Treading back into my bedroom, I glanced at the digital clock on my bedside table. It was half past four. I stretched out on the bed and gazed at the ceiling. Mary could be involved and still be innocent, I realized. In fact, it would probably be better for Howard if she were. I wouldn't know that, however, until I talked with her in the morning—and that was still several hours away. Closing my eyes, I tried to sleep, but the questions I wanted to ask her were already forming in my thoughts.

And if she weren't innocent? I said to myself. What would that mean?

Lying with my arms folded behind my head and gazing at the dark ceiling, I could feel my fragile sense of trust in Mary Leighton begin to melt like morning frost.

Twenty-Six

I dialed Mary Leighton's home number at a quarter past seven. When she heard my voice, she didn't seemed surprised. Waiting by the phone? I wondered. Her voice sounded cautious.

"I didn't think you were working on this story anymore, Donny," she said.

"I'm not, really," I replied. "I just have a few questions. Do you have a minute?"

She explained that she was busy getting her children ready for school. Then her son had a musical program at nine o'clock. She would be available to talk with me at noon.

"Would that be possible?" she asked.

"Fine," I said. "I'll meet you at your house."

Mary thought about this for a moment.

"Let's meet at Whitman's Book Shop," she suggested. "They have a few tables where we can get a cup of coffee or tea. It will be more relaxed."

"Okay," I said and hung up, knowing what she really meant—that it would be less obvious for her to be seen with a reporter.

Whitman's was another of my favorite places in Eden Springs. It was in the row of brick-fronted shops near

Nelligan's. Anne could never understand my interest in old books, but I found them fascinating. When you walk into a used bookstore, you never know what you are going to find. Wandering down the rows of old hardbacks was like exploring.

I arrived at Whitman's a few minutes early and sat at one of the four small round tables near the back window. There was no service here. You simply poured yourself a cup of coffee or hot tea and dropped a quarter in the basket. I poured myself a cup of coffee and sat down to wait. Mary arrived a few minutes later. She looked around as she pulled out her chair and shot me a nervous smile.

"Well. . ." she said and paused, as if she expected me to fill in the rest of her sentence.

"Thanks for coming," I offered. "Would you like some coffee?"

"With cream and sugar, please," she said.

We were being so cordial, I suddenly felt awkward. Did she consider this a hostile interview?

Tossing another quarter in the basket, I set Mary's coffee on the table. She smiled gratefully.

"I just have a few questions," I said, sitting beside her.

"But you're off the story, right?" she asked anxiously.

"Who told you that?"

Mary blushed. "I assumed—since I hadn't seen your name on any of the articles recently . . ."

"You're right," I admitted. "I am off the story—basically. But there are a few things—loose ends, you know—which are bothering me."

"Like what?"

"Mainly background stuff," I explained. "For example, your desk was by Drussell's office door, wasn't it?"

Mary nodded.

"Had your desk always been in that position or had you recently been moved?"

She looked surprised.

"As a matter of fact, Stan assigned me to that desk just a week before," Mary said. "But . . ."

"I'm not implying anything," I interjected. "I'm just trying to get a picture of how things worked."

"Okay."

"Do you know Clifton Howard?"

Mary shrugged. "Clifton Howard? The manager of Kaplan Construction?"

"Yes."

"He came into our office a few times."

"Did you ever speak to him?"

"Probably."

"Did you ever happen to overhear Drussell talking to Howard on the telephone?"

Mary sipped her coffee thoughtfully. "Sometimes Stan talked on the phone very quietly. Almost in a whisper, you know, and I thought that was strange. But I had no idea to whom he was talking. I assumed he was making a personal call."

"But you never heard him specifically talking to Howard?"

"No." Mary began to rub her fingers nervously. "Do you think Mr. Howard is in on this somehow?"

I nodded and looked around the bookstore. Two women were standing in the corner and talking about a book.

I turned back to Mary. "I don't know if this is any consolation, but I'm pretty sure I know why it happened."

"Really?" Mary asked, her face brightening. "Then . . ."

I held up a hand. "But I still don't know how."

"That's okay," Mary blurted. "If you know why, then it's only a matter of time until you discover the how."

"I hope so."

Mary glanced at her watch. "I need to go, Donny."

"Just one last question."

She looked at me.

"Did anyone ever ask you if you knew a reporter on the Banner?"

Mary looked confused. "A reporter?"

"Yes."

Mary shook her head. "No, not that I can remember."

"Okay," I said. "It was just a wild shot."

"About what?" she asked.

"Nothing," I replied.

When I returned to the newspaper office, I went to see Ed Thomas and explained my theory to him. He leaned back in his chair and smiled.

"A complicated setup like that in Eden Springs?" he mused. "I can't see that happening, Donny."

"Not even for $1.8 million?" I stressed.

He rubbed the top of his balding head. "Look, our job is to report the facts as they happen. Not to go chasing off on bizarre theories or speculations . . ."

"I agree, Ed. But what if something like this did happen? Hypothetically speaking?"

"Hypothetically?" he muttered. "Well, we could print it if we had verifiable evidence—not just your pencil drawings."

"Okay. Then I have to get something concrete."

"That's what I'm afraid of," my editor said. "I don't want to find you at the bottom of the river."

Pulling on my jacket, I walked down the street to the town square. The leaves of the sycamore trees were beginning to fall and blow against the war monument. The pavilion looked peacefully deserted. It had been cold in the morning as I walked to work, but now the afternoon was sunny and reassuring. I stood across the street from my apartment and gazed up at the bay window. I could see myself up there each evening, banging away obsessively on my keyboard. And for what? I wondered. Because I believed God had given me a desire or talent to be a writer? Was I a writer? Yes, but not in the way I believed God wanted me to be, I thought with frustration. I had tried again and again—with that family on the prairie, and then the missionary in Africa—and nothing had happened. Now I was involved in a complicated journalism story that was preventing me from getting any of my own work done. Maybe I should forget it, I told myself. There were only two choices, anyway. Either I talked to Clifton Howard and told him I knew the whole story, or I talked with Stan Drussell. And if they said nothing? If they gave no response, or guilt-ridden confession? That would be the end of it.

I decided to check my mail, so I crossed the street to Cleary's Watch Shop and opened the side door to my stairway. In my box there were two bills and a letter from a friend in California. My friend mentioned that his overseas mission needed a writer with journalism experience. Was I interested? It might require some travel.

I laughed and carried the mail up to my apartment. The light was blinking red on my answering machine when I opened the door. I pushed the button and was surprised to hear Mary Leighton's voice on the tape.

"I'm sorry, Donny, but someone did ask me if I knew a reporter on the Banner. Clifton Howard—last spring. I apologize. I don't know why I forgot about it. I've just been so nervous these past few months. Please forgive me."

"Of course," I muttered and pressed the "save" button.

Crossing the street to the square again, I dropped onto a park bench. I could linger here for a few minutes until the sun slipped behind the courthouse tower and the chill began to seep into my jacket. I needed some time to think.

The way I saw it, Clifton Howard had somehow managed to pressure Drussell into lying about Mary's phone call to Braynard Construction. I say "pressure," but it may not have been pressure. Perhaps Drussell's involvement was a test of loyalty within the militia unit. Or maybe it was something as sinister as blackmail. Perhaps Howard had something on Drussell—knew about something illegal that had occurred during their experiences in the woods. Had Drussell accidentally killed someone? I wondered. I would have to check the back records to see if anyone had been reported missing; especially someone who was thought to have been in the woods around Wingert Lake. Why else would Drussell, a career city government official, have become involved in a scam with federal racketeering consequences?

At the same time, Howard had somehow managed to make a call from Mary's line. Then he had put the pressure on me because he knew I was a friend of Mary's and would not investigate the story as ruthlessly, perhaps, as someone who was more objective.

As I was sitting on the park bench, a man and a little girl passed me. The girl smiled at me sweetly, and I smiled back. A car that had been slowly rolling up Sixth Street stopped at the curb, and a man climbed out. As I watched, he went to use the pay telephone on the corner. Was he lost, I wondered, or had he forgotten something?

The man did not spend much time on the telephone. Jotting down something, he quickly jumped back into his car and drove away. He must have been calling for directions, I told myself. I gazed at the phone booth and then at the thick black cable that ran from it to a nearby telephone pole. The lines ran off along Ash Street. Telephone lines, I muttered to myself and stood up. The sun was down now behind the courthouse tower, and I zipped up my jacket. I glanced at my watch. It was almost five. If I hurried, I had just enough time.

Twenty-Seven

I was waiting inside the door of the municipal building when Jim Hastings drove up in his squad car.

"I thought reporters worked nights and slept late," Jim commented as he came through the door.

It was half past seven in the morning.

"Never," I said, shaking his hand. "But if you're tired, I'll buy you a cup of coffee when we're finished."

"At least," he said.

I motioned to a man standing next to me. "This is Ben Smith. He's a lineman for the telephone company."

"Another extension phone?" Jim asked.

"Not quite," I said. "Follow us."

I led Jim through a door marked STAFF ONLY and down a stairway to the basement. Above our heads ran the heating and cooling ducts for all the municipal offices. The floor was concrete and painted gray. We went down a hallway to the power plant section of the basement and entered another door. On the wall inside was a large, flat box. A thick pipe ran into the box from the ceiling.

"I've never been down here before," Jim said, looking around.

"I hadn't either until last night," I said. "I tried to call you then, but you were out."

"So what's this?" he asked.

"Why don't you tell him, Ben?" I suggested.

The lineman tapped the box. "This is your telephone connection box," he explained. "When you . . ."

"Wait a minute," I interrupted. "Before we open the box, you need to look at something, Jim."

I pointed to a small padlock securing the flat, metal door to the box.

"See this?" I asked.

Jim nodded.

"Open it."

"It's locked, isn't it?"

"Try it," I said.

Jim touched the lock and it fell open.

"Hmmm."

"Someone has pried open the door and then . . ."

"I get it," Jim said, frowning.

Ben opened the door. Inside the box were hundreds of colored wires.

"These are the various telephone lines from the offices upstairs," he explained. "They're all numbered." He pointed to a wire. "See this? If you know what line you want to tap, you can clip into it here."

Ben pulled out a lineman's telephone, from which ran a wire with a clip. He snapped it onto one of the wires, put the receiver to his ear, and listened. Then he offered the handset to Jim.

"See what I mean?" he asked.

Jim put the phone to his ear and then pulled it away. "I can't listen to anything legally without a court order," he said.

"But you get the idea?" I asked.

Jim nodded and began to look angry.

"Now this is the line to Mrs. Leighton's telephone in the City Works office," the telephone lineman continued. He shone a penlight at one of the wires. "If you look at this closely . . ." He took out a magnifying glass, held it over the wire, and motioned to Jim.

Jim looked at the wire through the glass.

"You can just see those two little rips in the sheathing."

Jim studied the wire for a moment.

"One on either side?" Jim asked.

"Right," Ben said. "Those are made from someone clipping into the line."

Jim straightened up. "And could you make a call from here?"

Ben began to dial his handset. "I've just called our office. We have a number for a line test."

Jim listened to the handset again. "And this would register as a call from whatever line you've clipped into?"

The lineman nodded.

Jim Hastings shook his head. "So this is the way it happened."

"It looks that way," I said.

"Okay then," Jim said. "Don't touch anything else. I'll have the box dusted for prints."

"Ready for that coffee?" I asked.

Jim frowned. "Now I don't have time."

So who had made the call? Drussell was in his office. I didn't think Clifton Howard would have been foolish enough to be sneaking around in the basement of the municipal building. That meant it was probably one of their other friends. Also, whoever had done it had to know something about telephones; all that wiring was incredibly complicated.

Later that morning I made another call to the sheriff's office.

"Jim," I said. "I was just thinking that if you checked the backgrounds of Howard, Carson, and Milbradt, you might find that one of them had experience with . . ."

"We've already done that," Jim said.

"And?"

"Joe Milbradt was in the Army Signal Corps."

"Communications?"

"That's it."

"Well, then . . ?"

"I've sent a car out to pick him up for questioning. But it's really a shut case."

"Why?"

The guy who clipped into the telephone wire did a good job of wiping off the box on the outside, but he left a clear thumbprint on the inside of the door."

"And that was?"

"Milbradt."

"Finally," I sighed. "I'll call Mary Leighton."

"Not yet," Jim urged. "I know it's tough, but it would be better if we waited one more day."

At half past eight the following morning, I was waiting on a bench in the sheriff's office. Jim had told me they would be bringing in Clifton Howard at about that time, and I wanted to be there. Was it vengeance? I asked myself. I was a reporter. It was my job. But there was more to it than that. Joe Milbradt had already made a deal with the prosecuting attorney to reduce his charge from racketeering to trespassing and obstruction of justice if he would testify against Howard and Drussell. So he had spent the night talking. At one point, he became so nervous they thought he was going to have a heart attack and called for a doctor. But he was all right now—at least when it came to the judicial system. I could only imagine what his militia buddies would do to him once he was released.

The unit pulled up outside, and I watched as Deputy Sheriff Hastings and another officer helped Cliff from the back seat. He looked pale and lost. I thought I would feel pleased when I saw him, but that wasn't my reaction. Rather, I felt sad. All of us are tempted by corruption at times. Either we remain firm in our convictions or we give in for various reasons if the motivation is strong enough. Clifton Howard had fallen. There was nothing to feel pleased about.

"Would you like to make a comment?" I asked as they brought him up to the desk. He looked at me, but I don't think he saw me. Or if he did, his thoughts of anger were too deep to register on his face. His jaw was set, and the cold blue eyes were fixed as if he were contemplating something far off. Perhaps he was—the end of a life he had known in Eden Springs. That was over, certainly.

"So that's it," Ed Thomas muttered, reading over my shoulder as I finished my news story.

I leaned back from the computer. "The sheriff has enough evidence on Howard and Drussell now to press charges," I said. "And they are starting the bidding process on the Cottonwood Road project over again."

"How long did that last bidding process take?" the editor asked.

"At least three months."

"And then another two or three months before the work actually begins?"

"Right."

"So maybe by next year, we'll begin to see construction."

"Something like that."

Ed dropped into the chair next to me. "Sometimes I wonder if we really need another road widened, or additional improvements to what is already a nice town," he mused thoughtfully.

"I know what you mean," I said.

"It's one thing if you can't drive because of the potholes, or if a building needs renovation. But at what point does a town lose its charm?"

"Why don't you write an editorial about it?" I suggested. "Ask for letters from the readers. We have three months now."

"Yes," Ed said thoughtfully. "Maybe we've been given a reprieve here."

He went into his office and began typing at his computer.

So that was it, I told myself, and I picked up the telephone to call Mary Leighton. Our lives could get back to normal again.

Twenty-Eight

As always, however, our lives were more complicated than I could acknowledge. It was as if we moved in a series of multiple planes, each intersecting at one point or another. Tag had stopped taking the hits, but as the crash investigation came to a close, it seemed that we had not progressed. Rather than gaining from the experience, I felt we had only reverted back to the way things were in June. Maybe that was all we could hope for, yet I felt the necessity of movement. I had always dreaded stagnancy, had felt myself becoming depressed at the thought of perpetually doing the same things. And yet, out of choice, I stayed on in Eden Springs. So I came to realize that for myself, the movement had to come from within.

Maybe Tag felt that way too, because the incident on the bridge affected him in a way I had not anticipated.

The call came at half past midnight. I had just gotten to sleep, after spending the evening with Anne at a Lions Club dinner. Grappling around in the darkness for the telephone, I cursed under my breath. I hated when the telephone rang in the middle of the night because it always caused my heart to jump. I didn't mind being awakened; it was that I always associated late-night calls with tragedy. It had begun when the phone rang through our silent house at two o'clock on a December morning. I had heard it from a long way off as I slept snuggled under the quilt my grandmother had made for me. The telephone ringing was a chilling sound so late at night, as it bounced over the tile kitchen floor and down the carpeted hallway to my room. A moment later I could hear the sound of hurried feet in the hallway, the receiver lifting, and a groggy "Yes?" from my father. A chill had raced through my body, beginning in my lower back and spreading up to my shoulders. This was not normal, I had told myself.

Slipping out of bed, I tip-toed out to the hallway and gazed into the kitchen. My mother stood there with the telephone in her hand, her voice trembling, and her shoulders shaking. My father stood beside her in the darkness, the only illumination coming from a small blue night light above the stove.

I knew without being told that something had happened to Grandfather Graham. Something irretrievable and irreconcilable had occurred, and I could only stand there, skinny and young and helpless as my mother's grief began to show. Then, hesitantly, awkwardly, my father had reached up and put an arm around her. When she felt his embrace, she had leaned her head against his chest and begun to sob.

It was the only time I had ever seen my father hug my mother, or show her any sign of affection whatsoever. So I slipped quietly back into bed and lay there with my heart pounding, feeling that life had come very close on that cold December morning and touched me in a way that I would never forget.

It was almost December now as I fumbled with the telephone in the darkness, and my heart was racing again.

"Hello," I muttered, as I flicked on the bedside lamp.

"Donny, it's Melissa," a familiar voice said over the line. "I'm sorry to call you so late, but I need your help."

There are secrets in every family, and promises. Sometimes the promises are meant to heal rather than to hide, to shelter rather than to obscure. Melissa still thought of Sylvie as an innocent, and in some ways she was—if innocence is a state of mind, rather than of physical experience. They had taken a family trip to Padre Island when Sylvie was fifteen years old. I still shake my head in puzzlement that such a tragic event could have taken place on an island named after a priest. But that was the way it happened.

Melissa and Sylvie had gone down to the beach to sunbathe for a while in the late afternoon. It was a beautiful day, and the Gulf of Mexico licked up the sandy beach. The girls had spread out their towels and covered themselves with lotion. Melissa had brought along a radio. After a time Sylvie had grown bored of sunbathing and listening to music and wandered down to the water, wading in the surf and looking for shells.

Melissa called out to her younger sister, "Don't go too far."

Sylvie waved that she understood and bent down to pick up a shell. Then she continued on, and Melissa closed her eyes and felt the hot sun on her face.

When Melissa woke up, she realized that Sylvie had not returned. Shading her eyes, she gazed up the beach, but did not see the slender form in the blue swimsuit.

Melissa was concerned but not actually worried. Hurrying across the hot sand to the beach pavilion, she phoned their motel room. Her father said that Sylvie had not returned. He asked if there was a problem.

"No," Melissa replied. "I just fell asleep and thought maybe I had missed her."

"Don't get too much sun," her father had warned.

"We won't," Melissa said and hurried back down to the beach.

Earlier that day a student from Texas A&M had been beaten up by three young Hispanic males. The three young men had left the student by the roadside and headed for the beach. There they had come across a pretty young girl wading tranquilly in the surf.

As Melissa hurried up the beach, she saw a group of people gathered by the dunes. There seemed to be a problem. Instinctively, she let out a short gasp and began to run. When Melissa reached the dunes, she saw Sylvie lying on a lifeguard stretcher. The younger sister was wrapped in a blanket. Her face was battered and swollen. Her lip was bleeding. She clung helplessly to the broken strap of her swimsuit.

"Oh, honey," Melissa had exclaimed, beginning to cry. "Oh, babe."

Some families have a curious way of dealing with tragedy. Sylvie's parents decided that if they never discussed the attack, then they could pretend it had never really happened. Over a period of time, this pretending solidified into something more real than the truth itself, and they could eventually begin to believe that it *had* never happened. Once they reached this point—where the truth had been twisted into unreality—then they could tell themselves (if they cared to let these thoughts enter this far into their minds) that the story had been fabricated out of the juvenile minds of precocious girls.

Their younger daughter was still as innocent as ever. No one could make them think differently, and since no one tried—there being only our family who knew the truth—the attack was reduced to a fantasy.

"But Father," Melissa had spoken up. "Don't you think Sylvie should get some counseling?"

"For what?" her father had asked. "Sylvie is fine. She just needs some rest."

So Sylvie had spent a week in her room, rocking in a chair beside the window with her knees pulled up under her chin, and gazing vacantly out to the rainy April streets of Eden Springs.

That was her secret—if you could call an incident which had been thrust upon her, and forced from her, a secret of her own. It was as if the nightmares she experienced for months afterwards belonged to someone else. The hands that groped at her as she tossed in her damp sheets at night were not real hands, and the harsh voices that assaulted her verbally were only the whisperings of an aging and settling house.

When I tried to talk with her about it once, she began to gasp for breath, as if something very heavy had settled on her chest. She arched her back, her head up, and repeated pitifully, "I can't. I can't. I can't, Donny."

I quickly changed the subject, and within a few minutes she began to relax again, her breathing becoming easier. I wondered if her parents had ever seen Sylvie this way. If so, how could they keep her from getting counseling? I also realized, with sudden anguish, that I had only glimpsed a fraction of her pain. For one infinitesimal moment, I had gazed into the emotional upheaval that lingered behind those beautiful eyes. This was no teenage trauma, I told myself. This was a writhing anguish. It was much deeper than I had ever realized. It gave me a new understanding of what Sylvie had gone through. Only then could I sympathize with her parents' selfish attempts to distance themselves from the attack.

Now it was after midnight, and Melissa was on the telephone.

"Tag and Sylvie have broken up," my cousin explained as I rubbed my eyes.

"Broken up?" I asked. "But they're getting married next month."

"Not anymore. It's off. He told her tonight."

I wasn't thinking very clearly. "You mean, Tag broke it off?"

"Of course he did," Melissa said angrily. "I told you not to let him hurt her, Donny. And you promised. You promised me."

"Wait a minute," I urged. "Can't we take this a bit slower? The last I heard, they were doing fine. What happened?"

"Listen," Melissa said.

Sylvie had thrown a surprise party for Tag to celebrate his acquittal. It was held at her house, and Melissa had helped with the preparations. Anne and I had been invited, as well as four or five airmen from the base—two of whom had been in the search party with us at the bridge. Tag was in a good mood. He had saved a man's life and had his Air Force career re-established—all in one morning. Sylvie was happy and proud of him. The pressure was off.

As I heard it from Sylvie much later, after the party she and Tag had cuddled up on the sofa in front of the fireplace. The rest of the family had gone to bed. For some unknown reason, possibly because he was in such a good mood, or because he was still pumped up from the inquiry results, Tag had brought up the question I had asked him that night on the bluff.

"Donny made an odd comment a few weeks ago," he mentioned, gazing at the fire.

"About what?" Sylvie asked, snuggling up against him.

"He wanted to know if you had told me something."

"Oh," she said hesitantly.

"Do you know what he was talking about?"

Sylvie leaned back against the sofa. "Yes," she sighed, and then repeated more thoughtfully. "Yes."

"Is there something I should know?"

"That depends."

"What do you mean?"

"We all have an image, don't we?" Sylvie said honestly. "I see you one way, and you see me another."

"I guess so," Tag agreed.

"But the image doesn't always tell the whole story, does it?"

"No," Tag said. "From my experience, it rarely comes close."

Sylvie laughed bitterly. "I've tried to be the kind of woman I think God wants me to be. I've always tried . . ." She wiped a tear from her cheek with the cuff of her sweater. "But something happened along the way . . ."

Tag pulled her close to him. "You don't have to tell me this," he whispered. "It doesn't matter. Not at all."

"Really?" she asked.

"Yes."

She knew then that she had to tell him, as if his acquiescence had opened a dam within her, or broken the seal on a wall that she had been forcing back with strength of will for years. She had never really talked to anyone about

218 ~ G. Roger Corey

it—not even to her sister—in detail. Now it was coming, and she almost felt relieved.

"It's a burden I've been carrying far too long," Sylvie began. "It started when I was fifteen and my family took a trip to Padre Island."

She spoke softly and gazed at the blue and yellow flicker of the flames rising up from the logs. Tag kept his arm around her, and for the first time, it came out clearly, without emotion, without gasping for breath. Perhaps it had finally receded far enough into the past that she could distance herself. Or perhaps it was having Tag there and knowing that his affection was unconditional.

"We all carry around these scars from life, don't we, Tag?" she asked when she had finished.

He was quiet for a long time, and then he said, "For me, yes. But not for you. It isn't fair that you should have to carry anything around."

"And why you?" she asked.

He thought about this for a moment. "Because maybe I'm not good enough."

"For what?"

"For God."

That was the first inclination she had of his battle with spiritual understanding.

"What do you mean?" she asked.

Tag gazed at the fire. "Nothing. I'm sorry, Sylvie. I wish I had been there for you."

"That's what Donny says," she admitted.

"Well," Tag said, his expression somber. "Sometimes Donny and I think alike."

"Yes," Sylvie said. "Sometimes you do."

Twenty-Nine

S o the question is: Do we share our secrets with those we love—when the secrets are tragic—or do we spare them that decision? For it does come down to a decision: a choice of whether to disregard what we have learned and go on a journey of emotional healing together, or to begin the sometimes painful process of separation. And when do we know whether the information we have just conveyed is like a leaf floating aimlessly into a river, or a match set to last year's dry timber? Sometimes we don't know until the words have been spoken, and then it may be too late.

For several days after Sylvie had told Tag about Padre Island, he had been distant. There was never anything specific, but he always seemed to have something else on his mind when they were together. When she asked him about it, he replied that he was fine. But the following morning, she received word that Tag was back in the hospital. His mother had driven him up to the city the night before. Sylvie immediately drove up to the VA hospital to see him. Tag was pleased to see her, but upon his return to Eden Spring his mood changed.

They had gone for a walk along his street. Gardner is one of the more attractive older streets in Eden Springs, and the houses are set back from the curb in Victorian style. The street is lined with maple trees, and by late November the leaves had turned a brittle gold and blew like paper stars across the yards.

Sylvie told me later that Tag had opened the conversation very directly.

"I've been thinking," he said, gazing at the sidewalk. "Maybe . . ." he hesitated.

"What?" Sylvie asked.

"Well, maybe . . ." he sighed. "We're pushing things too fast."

Sylvie took his arm. "What do you mean?"

"The ceremony."

"Ceremony?" she asked, confused. "Do you mean the wedding?"

Tag took a long breath and exhaled slowly. "Yes," he said finally. "The wedding."

Sylvie had no reply. It was as if everything she had felt and planned and hoped for had somehow wilted within the time frame of a single step; as if she had begun the stride in total happiness and ended it, her heel striking the uneven concrete, in complete despair. Melissa had warned her about the beguiling but insidious charm of some men—though she had never imagined Tag to be this way. Sylvie suddenly wondered if she really knew this young airman who walked beside her. But perhaps she was overreacting, she told herself.

"We can put it off, Tag," she said compassionately. "You've been under a terrible stress. I can only imagine . . ."

"I'm not looking for sympathy," Tag muttered quickly.

"Then what?" she asked, desperately.

"I just need . . ."

"What, Tag?" Sylvie murmured. "What do you need?"

He kept his eyes on the sidewalk and said slowly, "To make things better."

"What things?"

"Myself."

Sylvie detected a subtle anger in his voice. Was it against her? she wondered. Or something else? And if so, what? She felt a sudden chill and pulled the collar of her coat up around her ears. "I'm getting cold," she said, shivering. "Maybe we should head back."

He had never let go of her hand, and even in turning he held on tightly. That must count for something, Sylvie had told herself. That must mean something. He has never let go. Even in the midst of telling me that he doesn't want to marry me—not now, anyway—he has never let go of my hand. There must be something in that.

They walked back to the house slowly, not talking, but with the understanding that a thousand thoughts of desperation and anguish were flying between and around them, as if the very leaves blowing along the sidewalk were words that could not be spoken.

"I'll drive you home," he offered when they reached his gate.

"No," Sylvie replied. "I need to walk. It's not dark yet. I'll be all right."

"Are you sure?"

"Yes."

She did not look back as she walked toward Thirty-fifth Street, but she could tell that his eyes were still on her and knew that if she turned she would see him standing there, leaning against the gate and watching.

There is no cause for tears, she told herself. He just got out of the hospital and is feeling tired. That's all it is, fatigue. It could affect anyone this way. Why, if I had gone through what Tag has been through lately . . .

But she could not finish that thought because she had been through her own trials, and knew that sometimes you never fully recover.

The churning anguish, the feeling that she had consumed broken glass, did not settle into her stomach until the next evening. Since the beginning of their relationship, Tag had always dropped by to see her on Friday evenings. Sometimes he came over with a pizza, or they went out for dinner. After a time he did not bother to phone ahead to let her know that he was coming. It was understood that he would be there when he got off work, and so he always arrived in his uniform—not having taken the time to go home first and change his clothes. Sylvie found some joy in this, that Tag did not want to waste a minute of time when he could be with her.

Now it was almost midnight on Friday evening, and she was gazing out of her apartment window apprehensively. Tag had not come over, nor had he phoned.

"It's beginning to rain," Melissa reported as she hurried into the apartment and hung her coat on a peg by the door. Her curly red hair glistened from the rain that had blown in from the west while she was driving across town. "I can't believe it's so late. We were decorating for the dinner party tomorrow night, and . . ." She glanced around the room. "Where's Tag? Did he leave already? I wanted to catch him before . . ."

Something in Sylvie's attitude caused her to stop.

"Sylvie?"

Sylvie did not reply but continued to gaze blankly through the rainstreaked window.

Melissa looked around the room. "Where's Tag?"

"I don't know," Sylvie whispered after a moment, her voice trembling.

Melissa did not have to ask the meaning of that statement. Sylvie always knew exactly where Tag was at any given moment. When asked, she would reply with muted assurance that he was bowling, or at a squadron function, or a training meeting, or out with Donny. She always knew.

Melissa had assumed this awareness was more than just curiosity or insecurity on her sister's part. It was the inseparable bonding of two people who had become intertwined emotionally, who seemed to breathe the same air and to think the same thoughts.

Now Sylvie did not know.

A sudden, maternal anger swept up within Melissa, and her cheeks flushed.

"You can't tell me," she said. "You can't . . ."

Sylvie remained silent.

Melissa began to pace the room. "Did he have the consideration to call you? Tell me that he at least called you."

"He told me yesterday," Sylvie replied. "Only I didn't really believe it until tonight."

"What did he say?"

Sylvie shrugged. "He said that he needed . . ."

Her voice trailed off in thought.

"He needed?" Melissa repeated. "What did he need?"

"To change," Sylvie said and touched the windowpane with her fingertip. She formed a T in the frosted glass. "To make himself better—or something like that. I didn't really understand. I only thought he was tired."

She pulled her knees up under her chin and began to rock.

This movement, the primal despair behind this action, which Melissa had seen so often in the days following

Padre Island, made her cringe. Hurrying over to the window, she put her arms around her sister.

"It's all right, honey," she said soothingly. "I'll call Donny and find out what is happening. I'm sure this is all just a misunderstanding. I know Tag loves you."

"I do too," Sylvie said and, reaching up to the window, wiped out the T with her palm.

So my telephone rang after midnight, and thoughts of that cold December morning so long ago sprang involuntarily into my head.

After listening to Melissa's anger slowly subside, to be replaced by incomprehension and regret, I promised that I would do something.

"This can't happen," Melissa said. "Not to my sister. She doesn't deserve this, Donny."

"Of course not," I said reassuringly. "I'm sure that Tag doesn't mean to hurt her. It has to be something else."

"But what?" she asked. "He told her he needed to change. Do you know what he was talking about?"

"No."

"Well, will you please find out?"

"Yes. I'll call you as soon as I hear something."

Melissa was quiet for a moment.

"I'm sorry to put you in the middle of this, Donny," she said, her voice muffled. "I know you didn't intentionally put them together. Whatever happens, I'm not blaming you."

"Thanks," I said, realizing that her absolution had come too late to keep me from feeling guilty.

Thirty

~

The following morning I drove over to Tag's house as soon as I got out of bed. I knocked on the door with some urgency, and his mother answered. She looked embarrassed and upset. When she saw me, she pushed open the screen door.

"Good morning, Mrs. Taggart," I said tenderly, for she seemed to be in a fragile emotional state. "Is Tag up yet?"

She removed a lavender hankie from the cuff of her gray wool sweater and shook her head.

"No, Donny, I'm afraid he's gone," she replied, twisting the hankie between her fingers. "I drove him to the station earlier this morning."

"The train station?"

"No, the bus station."

"At what time did he leave, Mrs. Taggart?"

She looked past me to the street, and her eyes began to tear. Perhaps she had been wondering about that very question herself, trying to determine at exactly what point her son, the boy she had raised, had departed and this new individual had taken his place. When is it that our children truly depart from us? I wondered, thinking of my own parents, and even my grandparents.

225

"At half past seven, Donny," she said, lifting her voice with sudden intensity. Perhaps she hoped I would run after Tag and fetch him back. There was always that possibility—that a friend could accomplish what a mother's love could no longer attempt.

I glanced at my watch. It was a quarter to eight. Tag was already on the road.

"He took the bus to the city," Mrs. Taggart added dryly. "From there he's flying to Nevada."

"Nevada?" I asked, surprised. "He's been reassigned?"

She nodded. "Mmm. That's right."

I had to think fast now. I looked out to the street and to my Trooper parked at the curb.

"What to do now?" I muttered under my breath. "What to do . . . ?"

Then an idea came to me.

"May I use your telephone, Mrs. Taggart?" I asked.

"Of course, dear," she said and opened the screen to let me inside.

I phoned Sylvie and told her I was coming over to pick her up.

"Is this about Tag?" she asked.

"Of course," I responded with irritation. "Now get ready. I'm coming over right now. I'll explain later."

"Okay," she said and hung up.

I looked at Tag's mother, waiting patiently beside the stuffed chair in the living room. "I apologize, Mrs. Taggart," I began. "There are a hundred questions I've been wanting to ask you about Tag, but I didn't know if it was my place."

"I understand, Donny," she said. "It has been a trying time for Richard. You are his friend."

"I'm going to try to catch his bus," I explained. "I'll take Sylvie with me."

Mrs. Taggart shook her head sadly. "He feels so . . . so . . ."

I didn't have time for a prolonged conversation.

"I have to go, Mrs. Taggart," I said abruptly.

She nodded again, and I ran out the screen door and down the steps. Tag's bus had been on the road now for twenty minutes. With a little luck, and if my Trooper didn't overheat, we could catch up to him by the time he reached Warrenton.

Sylvie was waiting for me on the curb outside her apartment. She jumped in, and I tore off across town. We passed the farmer's market on Third Street, which was always set out on Saturday mornings, and headed for the river bridge. It was a clear, frosted morning. Sylvie's eyes flashed excitement and fear as we rolled over the flat, murky water and headed northwest through the woods.

"I don't know," she murmured after I had explained the situation to her. "I don't know if this is the right thing, Donny. If Tag wants to leave . . ."

I swerved on a sharp turn and accelerated as the ground began to rise. We were almost out of the river valley now, and then the going would be easier.

"Under normal circumstances, I would agree," I said. "But things haven't been right for Tag since he came back from the Gulf. He's not thinking straight."

"Well, if he hasn't been thinking straight, then maybe . . ."

She hesitated and ran a hand nervously through her dark hair.

I knew what she was thinking. If Tag hadn't been acting normally, perhaps that invalidated everything that had happened to him in the past six months. I didn't believe this was true. I knew Tag—or at least I knew the Tag who had gone off to Desert Storm. Also, something else had been nagging at the back of my mind. And I thought, It is the little things, the phrase caught off guard, the seemingly irrelevant comment, that allows us to truly see into a man's heart, as if these minor bits and pieces were miniscule fragments of a much larger whole—a secret, interior self-concept through which a man lives out his life. Tag had let several of these little pieces slip during the past months, and I was beginning to have a better understanding of how they fit together. And if I was right, then it was absolutely necessary for us to catch that bus.

Fortunately, there was not much traffic on Route 9 at that time of the morning, so I was able to hit eighty on the plateau, which stretched west. We passed the river again, with the sandstone bluffs off to our left, and then came the flat fields of the plains. All the colors now were subtle forms of brown and gray. Even the sky was gray, and I wondered if God ever looked down on us and our tragi-cally self-complicated, comic lives and shed a tear. I thought of Him now as the bearded Almighty who reached out to touch man in the painting in the Sistine Chapel. It was as if I could see God reaching His broad arm across the gray sky now—stretching out His hand to touch the distant horizon. And who was there? I won-dered. When God's finger came to rest, to whom would He be giving life? Did it reach as far as a bus headed west on a back-country, two-lane highway? Or was He holding it, slowing the bus enough so that life could catch up with the young man inside?

"There's something I've got to know," I said to Sylvie. "That story Tag told me about Bear. It wasn't exactly correct, was it?"

"No," Sylvie replied, shaking her head. "Not exactly."

"Well, maybe it would help if I knew what really happened."

Sylvie gazed out the window at the passing fields. "It isn't so much how it happened, Donny," she commented, "but why he told you about it the way he did."

"Okay," I said. "So tell me."

Sylvie ran her hands through her hair again. Was this a new unconscious tic she had recently developed? I wondered. Or was she nervous? Probably both, I told myself.

"It wasn't Bear's idea to put the jet in the hangar," she explained slowly. "It was Tag's. He was the one on the tractor. Bear wanted to take cover."

"Oh," I muttered and began to understand Tag's guilt about Bear's death and how it helped him to know that Bear was in heaven. Saving the F16 had been Tag's idea, and it had gotten Bear killed.

"But he couldn't have known," I added. "It was a risk. That happens in war."

"I thought so too," Sylvie agreed.

"But Tag doesn't see it that way?"

"No."

"Why not?"

"For the same reason that he jumped in front of the train on the bridge. He never liked Roy Dwyer all that much. You must have realized that."

"I don't understand," I admitted. "He was trying to save the man's life."

Sylvie leaned back into her seat and sighed. "Think about it for a moment, Donny," she urged. "You know Tag. Think about motivations."

I was immediately thrown back to that summer evening when I had run into Mr. Cully in the town square. I had been thinking about motivations then as I listened to the summer band performance; about Tag and the crash investigation, and of balance—of the metaphorical action of putting one foot in front of the other as we tread with diligence over the traps of life, the depressions, sufferings, failures, and promises that make up our personal Via Dolorosa. That was the evening we had walked down to the Sixth Street crossing to watch the express pass through.

"Motivations?" I repeated.

"Yes."

Route 9 dipped into a small valley that was cold in the shade, and then we came into the gray-filtered sunlight again as we raced up the far side. I thought about Tag and his life—the experiences I knew about, at least—and suddenly a reason for his actions became clear.

"There's the bus," Sylvie said, sitting up.

We were about ten miles east of Warrenton. The bus had pulled off on a gravel clearing beside a farm road, and a young woman was descending. The driver was helping her with her bags. I screeched in behind them and jumped out. Sylvie waited in the car. There was nothing but rolling pasture on either side of the blacktop. The young woman gazed at me questioningly and then spotted a truck waiting across the road. Picking up her suitcase, she began to cross. The driver examined me curiously.

"You here to catch the bus?" he asked.

"I'm looking for someone," I replied. "It's very important."

"Who?" he asked.

"A young airman."

"Third row right," the bus driver said. "But be quick. We've got a schedule."

"Thanks," I said.

I ran up to the bus and tapped on Tag's window. His back was to me. He turned around in surprise, and I motioned for him to come out.

"Donny," he said. "What on earth are you doing here?"

"Looking for you," I said. "Sylvie's with me."

Tag's face suddenly clouded.

"We need to get going, sir," the bus driver called.

"Just a moment, please," I said.

Sylvie came around the back side of the bus, and I motioned for her to wait.

Tag looked at her.

"You don't have to do this, Tag," I said quietly. "You don't."

"Listen, Donny," he said. "You don't understand."

I nodded. "You're right. I didn't understand at first. But I think I'm beginning to, now. And it's unfair. It's unfair to you and to Sylvie."

Tag gave me a confused look. "I . . ."

"How many Scud missiles or trains will there be before you think He accepts you? How many? Will there ever be enough?"

"Sir," called the bus driver.

"And it won't work, you see, because it isn't necessary," I continued. "It never has been, and never will be. You haven't been rejected. Never. You're good enough right now—as good as anyone."

He looked away from me toward Sylvie.

"I'm going to have to shut the door," the bus driver warned.

"One second, please," I said to him.

Reaching into my pocket, I took out my keys and handed them to Tag. "Give me your bus ticket. I'll get off at Warrenton with your duffle."

"But . . ."

"C'mon. The bus is leaving."

Tag pulled the ticket from his jacket pocket and handed it to me. I grabbed it and stepped onto the bus just as the doors were closing.

"My buddy's not going on," I explained to the driver. "I'll use his ticket as far as Warrenton. Okay?"

"Whatever," sighed the driver. "Just as long as we can get going."

I took a seat by the window. As the bus pulled away, I looked back and saw Tag and Sylvie standing together beside my Trooper. The crisp morning light streamed across the cornfields toward them. Then they embraced, and, feeling guilty, I turned away and looked up the road.

Well, I told myself, I hadn't been on a bus in a while. Maybe I should just keep going until I reached Colorado.

Thirty-One

~

There are a few instances in our lives when the timing and the intentions of an action are matched perfectly, and that crazy dash up Route 9 to catch Tag's bus was one of them for me. It was the summation of everything that had happened to me during the summer and fall, of the things I had learned in those months, and of the relationships that had touched me.

My first reaction to Tag's departure was that he had been disillusioned about Sylvie's past. But the more I thought about it, the more I realized that his problem had gone back much farther than a few days. At some point in his life, Tag had been derailed from his relationship with God, and now I was beginning to understand when that had happened. During those nights he had spent praying for his father on the church steps—the nights he felt were wasted because God had not answered his prayers—Tag had decided that God did not love him enough, or that he was not good enough, to have his prayers answered. From then on, he had tried to win God's heart by playing the hero. It was an honorable and tragic gesture and, of course, one that was doomed to failure because you cannot win the heart of someone who has already given

234 ~ G. Roger Corey

their heart to you. It is unnecessary to gain someone's love when they already love you. The Lord had reached out across those gray wool skies that morning and slowed Tag's bus enough to allow us to catch it. And once he had seen Sylvie and spoken to her, Tag had realized his mistake.

That was on Saturday.

They were married the next afternoon in a small ceremony at the First Assembly Church. I served as best man. Melissa and Anne were the bridesmaids. Sylvie wore a beautiful wedding dress, with a lacy veil that Tag lifted when they said their vows. I watched self-consciously as he lifted the veil, and I sucked in my breath when I saw how beautiful she looked, her dark eyes gazing at him with so much tenderness and trust. As they recited their vows, they both seemed so innocent. I had assumed that Tag was drawn to Sylvie by her innocence, but perhaps it wasn't that way at all. Perhaps it was because she was able to tap something deep within him that was still innocent, a small corner in his heart which still believed in life as it was meant to be. After all Tag had been through, Sylvie was able to give him that gift.

Afterwards we drove out to the Rotary Club for the reception. We danced and laughed, and when they finally ran out to their car, the rice sprinkling down upon them, I thought, Please, Lord, let them be happy.

As their car pulled away, two F16s streaked across the evening sky and I thought, Yes, that's them, living a life now that is brighter than the light of one person and more impermeable.

When a friend once asked me if I ever regretted growing up in a small town, I quickly said no. But later I realized that this brief answer had been like the distillation not only of my life but of generations of my family. We all had grown up here, had passed the tempestuous days of our youth here, had learned the lessons of life and of God, and had felt the coal-black soot of passing trains blow into the air and settle on our skin. Grandmother Graham used to tell me, "Donny, this is the life the good Lord has given to us. We must try to make the best of it." So I was trying to live up to those expectations, though for me it was a daily struggle.

Perhaps if I had not grown up in Eden Springs, I would not have traveled to the same places or known the same people—but would I have been happier? Walking down these sidewalks, I could tell myself, This is where I kissed my first girl, and this is the ballpark where I hit a home run when I was twelve. My great-grandfather passed away in a rocking chair on the porch of that house; my grandparents walked home in the rain along this old sidewalk after they were married; my mother found a dollar bill in this gutter when she was fifteen, while she was sitting there crying because she had been invited to a school dance and wanted to get her hair cut; my father had broken his leg on that corner when a speeding car had hit his bicycle; this is where I graduated from high school, this is where I met Anne Perrault, and this is where I accepted Jesus.

Would I be the same person now if I hadn't grown up in Eden Springs? I wondered. Would I have the same thoughts and reactions and would my life have turned out the same? Some of the answers were obvious. How did the poem go? Yet knowing how way leads on to why.

I had remained in Eden Springs because I needed that feeling of stability, of being grounded in my family and heritage, of being from a place and of a place. And so that night I sat at my computer and wrote:

Chapter One

Some people hold sensitivity like a lantern before them as they move through life, and it only takes one glance to know how they will react to any given situation. With others, however, this quality is masked behind something elusive, and you are never quite certain where they, or you, stand. This is how I felt about Richard Taggart when he returned to Eden Springs from the Gulf War. We were not exactly a sleepy little community on the banks of the Missouri River—this was due to our close proximity to Emerson Air Force Base—but we were provincial, and Tag had just been overseas. I had known him since childhood, and although I could not at first comprehend the evasiveness of his actions, he did return with that same intensity of gaze—the set mouth, the furrowed brow—as if something important or necessary always conjured in the depths of his thoughts.

I worked all night on the chapter as Tag and Sylvie flew west to their new home in Nevada. And for the first time, I knew that I had written something that was not posturing or imagination but the truth as I understood it—of who I was, and where I had come from.

In the morning, I phoned Anne and asked her to wait for me because I was coming over

"That was so nice yesterday, wasn't it?" she asked sweetly.

"Yes," I replied. "It was."

I bought a bouquet of flowers at the corner store and jumped into my Trooper. There was a feeling of snow in the air as I drove out to Genesee Street, and the potato field was covered in frost. So winter had finally come, I thought to myself. But it didn't feel that way for me.

Anne was waiting just inside the door. I hurried up the steps with a big smile on my face. She looked at me excitedly as I held out the flowers.

"For me?" she asked.

"Yes," I said. "Will you?"

Anne gazed at me with a sudden swelling of emotion, and I thought, So it has been there all along, this feeling of wholeness.

God had planned it this way, and I had been too caught up in my own selfish desires to understand. There was no need for any more contemplation. The longing I had been trying to fulfill for years, the loneliness I had thought about so intensely that evening on the riverbank during the fireworks, was quickly filling up. In a moment it would be gone forever, and in the process I would be moving closer to the young men and women who had gone before me, because at one time they too had felt this way, had known this feeling of longing and seen it change to belonging. This was the way it was supposed to be. Tag and Sylvie had apparently understood. I had seen it the evening they were sitting on Tag's front porch and she had gazed up at me so serenely. They had not said anything, but perhaps it was not something you could communicate. Perhaps the understanding came only with the experience, and it made me wonder about spiritual truth and how much better we would understand if we had experienced it ourselves, had been there with Abraham, and Moses, and walked along the olive shaded paths with Jesus. Maybe there were some things in life that we could only truly understand through the process of doing them, and if so, then it was my turn.

"Yes," Anne replied, with tears on her cheeks.

The promise that had lingered in her touch and in the scent of her hair for so long had come true.

I took her in my arms. "I've started a new book," I whispered. "I've been up all night working on it."

"Really?" Anne asked, gazing up at me. "Does it have a happy ending?"

"Very," I said, and wiped the tears from her cheeks.